Dating THE INTERN

NATALINA REIS

Dating the Intern

Copyright © 2021 by Natalina Reis

Coordinated by: Hot Tree Self-Publishing
Editor: Hot Tree Editing
Interior Design: RMGraphX
Cover Designer: RMGraphX

Paperback ISBN: 978-0-578-84545-6

DEDICATION

I dedicate this book to our wonderful diverse world and the brave, resilient, and kind people that live in it.

FOREWORD

Those who have read some of my books know by now that I am a language geek. A linguist by trade, I'm fascinated by the intricacies and nuances of language. In this book you're introduced to Li Qiang, a young professional man from a Chinese background who once in a while uses his ancestral language, Mandarin, to express himself. I'm not a Mandarin speaker and the very few words or phrases I know do not remotely qualify me as an expert. I was lucky enough to conference with a native speaker to make sure I was using these words in the correct context and I'm having fun learning.

As a matter of pure curiosity and to help readers better understand some of the language within this story, I've compiled a tiny glossary of sorts not only of the few Mandarin words and phrases but also of a few expressions used in the online dating world today. I hope this makes your reading just a bit more pleasurable.

Please note that the pronunciation of the Mandarin words (in parenthesis) is only approximate

DATING VOCABULARY

Firedoorers- A one sided relationship in which one person is usually being taken advantage of.

Benchers - In short, a bencher keeps you in their rotation while playing the field, regardless of whether or not you're sitting there waiting and hoping for a monogamous relationship.

Cushioners - Basically, a cushioner is someone who keeps extra guys/gals on the side, mainly to boost their self-esteem and reassure them, just in case things don't work out with the main person they're pursuing.

MANDARIN WORDS AND PHRASES

Yātou (yah tah) - girl, used normally by a family member as a term of endearment but it can also be taken as condescending.

Nǐ hǎo (nee how) - hello

Duìbùqǐ (doo boo tchee) - I'm sorry, sorry

Mā (mah) - mom

Gūniáng (qoo nyah) - girl, a respectful, more formal word for girl, in the past was used as a title for a young unmarried girl

Shǎ gūniáng (shah qoo nyah) - silly girl

Bìxià (bee-shah) - Your Majesty (addressing royalty)

Wǒ ài nǐ (wah-I-nee) - I love you

Háizi (hi-za) emphasize the "h" sound like in the word hot - child

Wǒ de ài (wah-die) - my love

Xiǎoli (chao-lee) - literally "little Li", a nickname for an adult whose family name is Li

Wei're (way-er) or Qiang'er (chang-er) - affectionate nickname normally used by close family members. You add an "er" to the end of a first name.

CHAPTER ONE

STARDOM BOUND

This should have never happened. Of all the stupid things fate could have come up with, this one topped the cake. I stood there, phone halfway between my ear and the table, stunned out of the ability to move or speak. What the hell had just happened? I had never aspired to fame, being more than satisfied with a successful yet subdued life, perfectly happy blending in with the background, invisible in a crowd. Now, fame was seeking me out. It was freaking beckoning to me, and I, like a brainless butterfly, was answering its call.

When the phone rang, the number on the screen meant nothing to me. I contemplated not answering, but I did, afraid it was another entrepreneur interested in sponsoring or supporting my business. It wasn't.

"Ms. Tower, we have heard so many good things about your agency," a strange voice claiming to be a certain Mr. Robertson, head of programming for a local network channel, said in a sticky voice I instantly disliked. "We would love to feature you in a news spot next month." What? Why would anyone want to feature me and my online dating site? "We spotlight local businesses every week to show our support. Yours is very successful. We checked out your stats, and we're impressed by the rate of success you have with your love matches." The words sounded genuine, but the tone didn't. There was a creepy quality to the man's voice that made me cringe. "Ninety percent success rate is unheard of in this kind of business. Kudos."

I coughed up a thank you, not too sure I understood what he was saying. I did have an amazing success rate in matching my customers with life partners, most of which ended in marriage. The secret was not so much in a complicated algorithm but rather in personal advice and interaction between me, some of my employees, and the customers. At the Ivory Tower Agency, we worked extra hard to make sure our clients got their happily ever after. I had a team of people specially trained to ferret out the firedoorers, the benchers, and the cushioners. People who used our services to mislead others were swiftly dealt with and removed from the system, which in turn made our serious customers—those who were truly looking for the love of their lives—feel safe and happy.

"With springtime upon us, we would love to feature you and some of your customers in a special called

Spring Into Love," the slimy man continued. "We will not pay you for your trouble, but the exposure you'll get is priceless." I could use some free advertising. Even though we were doing well on the whole, our profit margin was pretty narrow, and I often struggled to make ends meet. For the kind of services we offered, I needed lots of hands on deck, which cost money. I started employing interns willing to be paid a nominal salary in exchange for the on-the-job experience, but with the business growing as it was, the need for more employees had also grown.

I was tempted. "What exactly would it entail?" I asked, my red-alert, run-for-the-hills alarm fighting with the wish to get some free publicity.

"Nothing much." Why did he sound as if he meant the opposite? "A couple of interviews with you, an employee or two, and a few customers. Then we will have you make a live appearance on the news." I sucked in a breath, the idea of being on live TV too terrifying to contemplate. "It will be very low-key at an ungodly hour of the morning when very few people will be watching." Was he trying to encourage me to do it or the opposite? How would an appearance on a show no one would watch help my business? He seemed to have read my mind. "It will be replayed later in the day during prime time so anything that goes wrong can be edited out before airing the second time. You will get great exposure."

Needless to say, I said yes. Not even five minutes

later, the magnitude of what I had just done hit me like a hammer on a nail. *Holy shit! I just committed to be on live TV.* Me, who couldn't even stand to look at pictures of myself without wanting to crawl into a giant hole in the ground.

The strident screech of my doorbell snapped me out of my paralysis. *I really have to change that stupid bell.* I set the phone down on the cocktail table and strode to the door, rising on my tiptoes to look through the peephole. It was Amber Lee, my best friend and general manager who had been with me from the very beginning of my venture into the online dating business.

Unlocking the door, I opened it to allow my friend to mosey on inside, her usual lazy smile stretched across her lips. "I heard," she said, throwing her tiny purse onto the couch and setting both hands on her wide hips. "It's about time you step out of your comfort zone."

I closed the door and ignored her, stepping away and throwing myself nonchalantly after her purse on to the soft, overstuffed sofa. "No big deal." My words belied the tightness in my gut, the hand of anxiety closing around my stomach. "It's an early, short appearance. I won't even have to talk much at all." Or so Robertson claimed. "I just have to sit, smile, and look pretty." I could do the sitting and the smiling, but I wasn't sure about the looking pretty part. I was certainly no beauty with my five-foot-three height, plain brown hair and eyes, and freckled face. At most, I could pass for an ordinary-looking woman with average looks.

Amber Lee's burst of laughter made me want to throttle her, but I reminded myself she was my BFF and that life would be pretty bleak without her by my side. "Don't give me that fucking crap. You're terrified, and you know it."

The thought tugging at my mind since she walked in finally coalesced into something I could make sense of. "Wait! How do you know? I just now talked to Robertson." I narrowed my eyes at her as she made herself comfortable beside me.

Her sky-blue eyes twinkled with mischief. "I have a friend at the TV station who told me he was going to call you." I opened my mouth to ask her something else, but she cut me off. "How did I know you accepted it? You may be a chicken when it comes to being the center of attention, but you are a good businesswoman, and I knew you would never pass on a chance like this." She knew me too well. "So close that gaping mouth of yours and fill me in on all the dirty details."

We spent the next hour or so talking over what the creepy TV guy told me while stuffing our faces with the heavenly dark chocolates a client had brought me from Belgium a week ago. It was always easy to talk to Amber Lee who was painfully honest sometimes but also deeply compassionate. She kept me real when I tended to lose myself in flights of fantasy.

"How did the date with Ben go the other day?"

I was afraid she would ask about that. Things had

not gone well. During our date at a fancy restaurant, I spaced out after the first ten minutes of conversation about how well his favorite hockey team was doing and planned out a whole new marketing strategy for our company in my head. Needless to say, he noticed I wasn't into him when I answered all his questions with a noncommittal uh-huh and a nod of the head. But to give him due credit, he didn't catch on until the end of the date; I guess he mistook my dreamy expression for interest.

"We won't be going out again," I said as quickly as I could, hoping she wouldn't notice. She pinched her lips and opened her eyes so wide, I thought they would pop out of their sockets. "Don't be mad. All he wanted to talk about was hockey. We would bore each other to death within the first couple dates."

"You're too freaking picky for your own good. You will never find a man that way." I wasn't that interested in finding a man—or at least not for the sake of dating. At heart I was a true romantic, still believing there was one person perfect for everyone. I just hadn't found mine yet. "You dish out all this romance advice to your customers when in fact you have no idea what you're talking about. How long has it been since you dated?"

"Not that long." My most recent boyfriend had been long gone since his break-up text six months ago. At that time, I hadn't seen him in almost two months while he traveled in Northern Europe, getting high and laid every chance he got. "I'm too busy for guys."

Amber Lee huffed and folded her arms over her generous breasts. "You're full of shit. You need to follow your own advice and put yourself out there." Not much chance of that. I was a homebody who hated to make small talk and got tongue-tied when speaking to people I didn't know well. Talking to clients was different, there was a conversation map, so to speak. We were quiet for a moment. She unfolded her arms and sighed. "All right, I won't fight with you anymore. Espresso?"

I nodded, and she stood up to go brew us some coffee. I hugged a cushion, my chin resting on the edge. I was lonely but resigned to spending the rest of my life flying solo. I always admired and envied other women who seemed so at ease in social situations, with just the right thing to say hanging on the tip of their tongues at all times. I was the one who hid in a corner, glass of nonalcoholic beverage in hand, wishing someone would come to engage me in conversation with the same ferocity as wishing everyone would leave me be. I was a pain in my own ass, so how could I expect others to think otherwise?

My friend returned from the kitchen—or coffee heaven, as I liked to call it—with the tiny cups in her hand. "Guess who just won a literary award this week?"

I stretched my hand to take my coffee from her. "J.K. Rowling?" Yes, I was a huge fan of everything Harry Potter. The coffee smelled heavenly, so I took a long sniff.

"Your intern." I looked up from the coffee, raising my eyebrows. "Li Qiang. That boy is amazing."

Li Qiang started working for me a couple months back. The man had an incredible resume for someone that young. Only twenty-seven, he already had a master's in business, two published novels, and now a prestigious award it seemed. "Wow, not sure whether to be impressed or jealous." I couldn't understand why he would want to work as an intern in a company like ours, but I was not about to turn down a good deal. Not to mention that he was very easy on the eyes.

Amber Lee sat next to me again, twitching her nose like Samantha from *Bewitched*. "He's handsome and brilliant," she said in a tone that suggested a hidden meaning. She wiggled her eyebrows at me, and I furrowed mine, totally confused. She sighed loudly. "You're so thick, girl. I was trying to imply that you should go for him."

My jaw dropped, and I choked on my espresso. "What the hell, Lee Lee? I'm not that desperate for a date." I put my coffee down and threw a pillow at her.

She laughed. "Right, because it would be such a sacrifice to date a young, hot, brilliant guy." Just because it was true didn't make it right. "I don't know how you'd bear it."

I humphed and made a face at her. "He's almost ten years younger than me and would never in a million years even consider dating little old me." Not that I'd want it. I was perfectly happy being single.

"So you're telling me you haven't noticed how beautiful Li Qiang is?" Of course I'd noticed. The man was… I didn't quite have words to describe him. He was tall, a couple inches over six feet at least, and had the most kissable lips I had ever seen in a guy: full and perfectly shaped. I'm not going to lie; I may have daydreamed about kissing him once or twice. "I've had a few wet dreams about him."

Heat rose to my face so quickly I didn't have time to hide it. *Damn you, Amber Lee. Leave it to you to make me feel like a teenager again.* She smirked, satisfied with the reaction she snagged from me. "You're evil, my friend. Yes, I've noticed his hotness, but he's super young and my underling." As soon as I said it, I cringed at my choice of words.

"Underling? Who says that?" I had fallen straight into her trap. Damn it. She chuckled. "This is why dating a younger guy would do you good. You need to catch up with the times, woman."

She might have a point there, however small, but I wasn't going to date anyone—Li Qiang or anyone else—just because I was lonely. Wait! Shit, I *was* lonely. I hated when others knew more about me than myself. They probably pitied me, the successful thirty-six-year-old woman with no one to love. How embarrassing.

Thanks to my meddling friend, I couldn't stop stealing

glances at Li Qiang from behind the large window that separated my small office from the rest of the space. I found myself wandering over to the glass half wall and watching him from behind my lashes all the while pretending I was reading. At one point, Amber Lee stuck her head through the gap in the doorway to warn me the book in my hands was upside down. She laughed, and I blushed—nothing new there.

"Boss, you have a visitor." Marianne, a perky young woman who had been working for me for almost a year, squinted at me from the open door. "Should I let her in?"

I was deep into a customer's profile. I raised my head and blinked a few times before her words sank in. Who could that possibly be? No one ever visited the office. Even the customers met with us elsewhere. "Who is it?" Curiosity bloomed inside me.

"Someone from the local news channel," she said, still squinting. Where were her glasses? "Teresa something-or-other." I really should train my staff on how to take messages. Maybe it was time for me to get a secretary.

I closed my laptop and nodded. "Bring her in." My employee turned around to leave. "Oh, Marianne, can you bring a water bottle and a glass for the visitor?" Marianne looked at me as if I'd grown two heads. I *really* needed to train my staff in public relations. I made a mental note to talk to them about this at our next staff meeting.

Seconds later, a tall, gorgeous woman walked in my office. She had to be a model, her blonde hair perfectly coiffed and a dress that hugged every inch of her sexy curves. Was she even real? Her lips stretched into a friendly smile. "Sorry to barge in like this," she said, offering a limp hand for a shake. "I was going to call, but I thought face-to-face would be so much more personal." As long as I didn't have to chitchat, I was okay with it.

"What can I do to help you?" I pointed toward the two comfy stuffed chairs at the corner of my office. She sat down just as Marianne, still squinting, walked in with the water. "Can I offer you coffee or tea?"

She shook her head. "Thank you, but water is fine."

I took the seat on the next chair and folded my hands on my lap, waiting. Marianne set the water down on the small table between the two chairs and left, but not before giving me a look that said, "Who is this doll?" I almost laughed.

"You must be wondering why I'm here." The little flame of curiosity had turned into a full tundra fire. "I work for programming at the TV station, and Mr. Robertson put me in charge of the details for the *Spring Into Love* spot. We have received the signed contract, thank you very much for being so prompt." I had to be, otherwise I'd forget. That was a strategy I'd learned as a kid—do what you have to do right away before your brain puts it in a dark, forgotten room in your mind.

"Was there a problem with it?" It was a pretty

standard, no-frills legal document that made my agreement to be featured on their news official.

She laughed softly. "No, no problem. I just want to go over some of the specifics. We have your professional bio, but we need something a bit more personal." I startled a bit at that. How was my personal life of any interest? "The public loves to feel as if they have an inside look into your life. Don't worry. We don't have to give them anything terribly private, but it will help if it's something that is directly connected to your job—in your case, the matchmaking services."

I was confused, and I was sure it showed because she tilted her head as if assessing whether I was fooling around or just plain stupid. "I'm sorry. I don't quite understand what kind of information you're looking for."

"Your love life." What? What was she talking about? "You're the CEO of a successful matchmaking company who stands out from others because of the personal interaction with your clients, the advice you give them. You have a special insight into the world of dating and romantic relationships, which is what makes your services so successful." I was still confused, and I furrowed my eyebrows in response. "In other words, we need information about your love life. We'd love to meet and interview your SO."

What fresh kind of hell was this? "You want me to do what?" I was so shell-shocked I forgot to hide my surprise.

She raised her hands in a reassuring gesture. "Don't panic. It won't be anything too personal, just a matter of bringing your boyfriend along—I'm assuming you're not married—and answering some simple questions about your own relationship."

"What kind of questions?" What I should be asking was "What boyfriend?" but I was too stunned to think straight.

"You know, where did you meet, how did you know he was the one, are you planning a wedding soon… simple stuff." Simple enough for someone with an actual boyfriend.

"What if I don't have a SO?" Which I didn't.

"That would look really bad for you and your company," Teresa said, her lips cutting a small smile again. "How can someone without a romantic relationship dish out advice on it? You would lose the trust of your clientele." She gave me a sideways glance. "You're just being coy, right? You do have a fiancé or at least a boyfriend." *Oh, you have no idea of how much I'm not bullshitting you.*

I swallowed the large knot in my throat and discreetly wiped a few beads of sweat collecting on my forehead. "Of course I have a boyfriend." I forced a smile that probably looked more like a frown. "I just don't like to air out my private life in public."

She slapped her own thighs. "Perfect. Everyone will be curious about your own romance, so we'll give them a slice of it. Perfect." Far from it. Not perfect at all. I was stuck between a nonexistent boyfriend and a legal contract that may mean a much-needed boom in business.

What the hell had I just got myself into?

❤ ❤ ❤

"Ms. Tower." It was a disembodied voice, and for a moment I wondered whether our office was haunted. That was until I realized I had been covering my head, sandwiching it between the hard top of my desk and the muffling softness of a large cushion. I loosened my hold on the pillow and pulled it aside, slowly adjusting my eyes to the brightness of the room. "Ms. Tower?"

My eyes first met a pair of jeans, hanging low on a male's narrow hips, and then followed the whiteness of his shirt, stretched taut over his chest and all the way up to his beautiful face. God, he was gorgeous! For a moment or two, I pondered on my impulse to wrap my hands around his waist and pull him against me. Then I realized who I was lusting over in my office and that my messy bun had somehow turned into a rat's nest while hiding underneath the pillow. I hastily brushed my hair with my fingers, undoubtedly making it look even worse, and jumped to my feet, hoping to God I didn't have spit dripping from the corner of my mouth.

"Yes?" It was a croak rather than a word. I cleared my throat, heat burning my cheeks. "What's the problem?"

Li Qiang's luscious lips stretched into a lazy smile. "Sorry to wake you up from your nap," he said, hiding a chuckle behind his hand.

I smoothed out possible crinkles on my blue dress and licked my lips. "I wasn't sleeping," I protested, louder than the situation warranted. "I was… meditating. My yoga teacher told me to do that a few times during the workday." Not a total lie; my instructor did say that to me, but I was obviously just having a shut-eye to block my problems away. When everything else failed, I tried to ignore it. My lifelong, fail-proof strategy wasn't working this time.

"You look stressed," he said, with what sounded like genuine concern in his voice. "Is everything okay? Can I help with anything?"

I didn't know if it was the look he gave me, the fact that I had indeed kind of just woken up from a weird dream, or the whole nonexistent boyfriend fiasco, but I lost it. I burst out crying. Not just crying, ugly crying. Thankfully, I hadn't gone crazy with the mascara that morning or the raccoons would have nothing on me. The poor intern looked as lost as I was out of control, his hands hovering close to my shoulders and arms but not actually touching. His lips were pressed so close together, they had lost all sense of shape. If I hadn't been so hysterical, I would have felt sorry for him. As it was, I couldn't stop feeling sorry for myself, and in the back of my mind I knew I would be mortified later, but all I wanted—all I needed—at that moment was a strong shoulder to cry on, and his was the only one available. Much to his dismay, I'm sure, I dropped my head to his chest, as close as I could get to his shoulders, and allowed the waterworks to continue.

The tears fell for a long time, punctuated ever so often by little sobs that I couldn't hold in. I lost track of time and my dignity as I stood there, leaning on a man I barely knew and who was my subordinate—worse yet, who was much younger than me.

As soon as the tears finally dried out, I became acutely aware of his hard pecs underneath my face and the awful, snotty stains on his immaculate shirt. "Oh my God. I'm so sorry," I said, in a panic, trying to brush the dark spots with my hands. Holy mother of God, it looked as if I was caressing him. I pulled my hands away, horrified. "Double sorry. I don't know what got into me. So, so sorry." Scared of looking at his face, I stared straight at the ugly blotches on the white of his shirt. "I'll buy you a new shirt. How unprofessional of me."

Before I knew what was happening, he held on to my hands. His were large and warm. I had the insane thought that my tiny, puny hands belonged in his. I couldn't avoid it any longer; I looked up at him. "Stop fussing. It's okay." He bent his head just enough to look me in the eyes. "Everyone has bad days. I'm glad I was here when you needed a good cry."

I sniffed like a little girl. "But your shirt… I made a mess out of it." I was glad he was holding my hands because I would have touched him again. I'd taken a total leave of my senses. "There's mascara all over it."

He clicked his tongue in an oddly old-fashioned way. "Nothing that won't wash out. Will you stop worrying about my shirt and tell me what's going on?"

I shouldn't. I really shouldn't confide in him. But he would be gone in a few months once his internship was over and I'd most likely never see him again. Who better to vent out my frustration about this whole mess? So, I did. He led me to the comfy couch and never once let go of my hands while I spilled out the whole silly and embarrassing story about the TV show and a boyfriend that didn't exist. At the time I didn't think anything of it, but later it hit me how gentle and sympathetic he was, listening to my torrent of complaints—whining, really—without interrupting other than offering the occasional nod.

"So you see," I concluded, feeling surprisingly better, "in a nutshell, I'm screwed." I hung my head, heavy with the realization I was in a seriously tight spot.

Li Qiang was quiet for a moment, and I didn't dare look at him, afraid of what I might read in his lovely eyes. When he squeezed my hands tighter, I almost jumped off my seat. "It's not as bad as you think," he said, and my chin jerked up. What did he mean exactly? "I have a plan, if you're willing to hear me out."

A plan? Of course I wanted to hear him out. A plan was better than what I had, which was nothing, zip, nada. I nodded frantically. "You do? What is it?"

"Don't freak out, okay?" He locked those awesome peepers with mine before continuing. "What if I pose as your boyfriend?"

Good thing I was seated, or I would have fallen on my ass. What was he saying? Was I hallucinating, or had he just offered himself as a sacrificial lamb? A beautiful, young, and smart one? "What did you say?" My voice went down a couple octaves; my mouth was as dry as a raisin left out in the sun for a while. "You posing as my what?"

A smile bloomed on his lips. "Your boyfriend," he repeated as if that made more sense the second time around. "I will pretend I'm your SO, and we'll play act for the world. Problem solved."

I coughed, and he offered me a sip from the bottle he'd brought in with him. "That's insane," I managed to squeak out. "Not fair to you and pretty risky for everyone involved. I mean, I don't even know you other than your name and that you've won a book award." I looked up at him in an attempt at a smile. "Congrats on that, by the way. I'm impressed."

He shrugged it away. "No big deal." Yes, of course it was a big deal, but I let it go for now. His proposal was still ringing in my head. "We still have a few weeks to get to know each other. We can practice so that we look and sound genuine." His smile was contagious; my lips stretched into what I was sure was a ridiculous grin. "Well, do we have a deal?"

My head moved of its own accord to agree with his insane idea. It looked as if I had just dug myself even deeper into that dark hole. The silver lining was I got to play girlfriend to that handsome man. This could turn out to be a total disaster, so why was I smiling from ear to ear?

CHAPTER TWO

DIGGING A HOLE

"You did what?" Amber Lee had her mouth open like a fish out of water. The news of my deal with Li Qiang had left her speechless—at least for a few seconds. My busty, curvy friend dropped to a chair and shook her head. "I must get my ears checked. I thought I just heard you say Mr. Hottie is going to pretend to be your boyfriend."

I'd invited her out to lunch so I could break the news in private. Knowing my friend, I could expect loud expressions of either dismay or excitement. I was right. Amber Lee was speaking so loudly, several patrons in the coffee shop stopped what they were doing to focus on us. Good thing I picked a shop we didn't normally frequent.

"Stop making a scene, Amber Lee," I told her, checking the tables around us. "Yes, I did say that. It was his idea."

For once she was quiet, her lips pinched and eyes dangerously shiny. This wasn't going to be good. "*He* offered? To be your fake boyfriend until after the show?" I nodded, grateful she seemed to be taking it a lot better than I thought she would. "How does he suggest you get to know each other well enough that it appears like a real relationship?"

Uh-oh. Right. "He says we have some time to get to know each other well enough," I whispered, a sheepish smile pulling on my lips.

She burst out laughing, a belly roar of a laugh that had everyone in the shop staring at us. "He's into you." What? I shook my head with gusto. "Oh yes, he is. Why else would he do that? If he has a girlfriend—which I can't believe that sexy ass doesn't have—it will be the end of the relationship." My eyes popped wide open. "Would you stay with a guy who is playing boyfriend and girlfriend with another woman?"

No, I wouldn't. Did that mean he was single too? Hard to believe, judging by the way every female in the office acted around him. "Maybe he's gay." *Oh please, God, don't let it be so.*

"Gay, shegay." She was always saying things like that. I always thought she should have been Dr. Seuss's cowriter. "I've seen the glances he throws at you when you're not looking. He's not gay."

"He is being nice," I said with less conviction. "He saw how upset and worried I was and decided to help out his boss." Technically, I wasn't really his boss, I guess, but I did pay him a small salary. The more I talked about it, the worst it sounded.

Amber Lee leaned over, bracing herself on her knees. "How are you going to explain this to the rest of the staff?" I deflated completely. Shit, I hadn't thought of that. They would know we were talking bullshit since Li Qiang and I had barely said ten words to each other since he started his internship with us. My friend placed a hand over mine. "Don't be so upset, girl. I think this is just what the doctor ordered. Fake or not, you'll be hanging out with a young guy instead of spending your nights with your nose buried in a book or watching one of those foreign shows on Netflix."

Fire erupted on my neck and cheeks. I was so pathetic, a thirty-six-year-old woman who was obsessed with young adult novels and manga-inspired series on TV. If on the surface I looked all put together and sure of myself, inside I was really a mess.

"Is this going to be the biggest mistake of my life?" I asked my friend, my forehead in my hands. Doom and gloom filled my heart. The TV people would figure out the lie and put me out of business, I was sure of it. "I should just call Mr. Robertson and admit my lack of love life."

Amber Lee grabbed my hands and gave me a stern look. "You won't do any such thing," she said. "This will be a fun experience for you." Yeah, if I was a masochist, which I was not. "And a great opportunity for your business. So stop moaning and enjoy the fact you will be glued at the hip—or hopefully other more fun body parts—with a hot, young hunk of a guy." Not for the first time, I wished I was more like her: fun loving and uninhibited. Instead I was the extra cautious one, always second-guessing myself and guilt-ridden about everything. Gah, I hated myself sometimes.

We drank our coffees and ate our sandwiches in silence, me bemoaning my stupidity, Amber Lee purely enjoying the deliciousness of her meal. When we were ready to leave, my friend turned to me and asked simply, "When are you guys meeting for the first time to talk things over?" I didn't know. We hadn't gone that far in our planning. I was guessing we would decide sometime in the next few days. After all, we worked together. "Lord, give me strength! You haven't even committed to a date to meet?" She rolled her eyes. "This is going to be interesting."

Interesting was not the word I would have chosen. Disastrous would be much more appropriate.

That afternoon I discreetly searched for Li Qiang, but he seemed to be MIA. When I thought no one else would hear, I asked Marianne, who always knew everyone's whereabouts, where he was.

"He had some work errands to run," she said. Then she squinted, her already small eyes shrinking to almost nothing. "You told him to do that last week, remember?" I didn't. But then again, I was lucky I could still remember my name after this whole fiasco.

"He'll be back before closing." All right, I'd talk to him then. Amber Lee was right; we needed to work on a plan, pronto.

If you asked me what I did for the rest of the day, I wouldn't be able to come up with anything. My eyes kept roaming over to the front door every time it opened, my anxiety rising every time someone else came through it. When he finally walked in, his backpack draped over a shoulder and still wearing the makeup-stained shirt, my heart skipped a beat. His eyes met mine and he waved, a generous smile lighting up his face.

"Li Qiang, can you come to my office, please?" I called out from my door, feeling utterly ridiculous and exposed even though no one gave a shit. He strode across the space toward my office and closed the door behind him. I walked around my desk and sat on my chair. Better if I kept this professional. *But how can you keep fake dating professional?*

He sat across from me, dropping his bag on the floor beside him. "We should meet outside work to discuss things, right?" Great, he could read minds too. "Are you free tomorrow evening?" It was Saturday, and I didn't have anything planned. I nodded. "Shall we meet at Beans & Brews?" I loved that coffee shop. "It's one of my favorite places to hang out. We can meet elsewhere if you don't like it."

"No, I really love it there." Uncanny that we actually had something in common. "Do you go there often? I've never seen you."

My eyes followed his tongue as it slid over his plump, wine-colored, kissable lips. Much to my mortification, I gasped and then tried to disguise it by rearranging the desk items in front of me.

"I go there almost every day after work to write."

Music to my ears; I love to read, he loves to write. A match made in heaven. Wait! What the hell was I thinking? *This is not a real relationship. Not real.* How did I go from "he's too young" to "he's my soul mate" in less than a day? Stress, this was all due to stress. A good night's sleep and my temporary madness would clear away.

"What do you write?" Shameful, really that I'd never taken the time to find out. Fake boyfriend or not, he'd been working for me for two months already. You'd think that a bookworm like me would be interested in something like that. Maybe it was my self-defenses protecting me from getting too interested in someone who was out of reach for me.

His eyes twinkled like stars. "Mostly fantasy. A bit mainstream, but I enjoy making up new worlds." Another thing in common, I loved reading fantasy. Damn. This couldn't be good. "I know you like to read." He swiped a hand in the air toward my book-laden shelves.

I actually giggled. I hadn't giggled since I was thirteen. "You should see my shelves at home." Shit. That sounded a lot like an invitation, didn't it? *Snap out of it, woman. You're an adult, independent female. This is not your first rodeo.* Except it felt like it was. Might as well be honest. "I do love fantasy, even though I'm a pretty eclectic reader."

He narrowed his eyes as if studying me. "I'd love to see your collection." Was that an invitation? Chitchat? I-want-to-be-your-love-slave confession? I shook my head, trying to dispel all those idiotic thoughts. He stood up suddenly. "Ms. Tower, we're on for tomorrow evening, right?"

I always forgot how tall he was, all slim muscle, so I stayed put, staring up at him in fangirl-like awe. "Considering we're about to announce to the world we are a couple, maybe you should just call me Ivory." First sensible thing I said all day.

He swung his backpack over a shoulder and offered me one more of his lovely smiles. "See you soon, Ivy."

I watched him leave my office, confidence oozing from every step, and I sighed. *He gave me a nickname.*

♥ ♥ ♥

Beans & Brews was a favorite place of mine. It stood where an old new-age store had been. The owner, a modern witch, had turned it into a space where you could have a great cup of tea or coffee, eat a healthy sandwich or soup, and browse the shelves for just the right amulet or magic trinket to make you happy. The place was well frequented, even late in the evening.

Most of the tables were occupied by people either glued to their laptops, earbuds attached to their heads, and minds elsewhere, or busy eating café sandwiches and drinking fancy coffees while browsing the web on their phones. By some kind of miracle, I had managed to secure a two-person booth in a darker corner of the coffee shop and busied myself by obsessively tapping my fingers on the large white mug that held a cappuccino. Every minute or so I checked my phone for messages. Li Qiang was not late. I had arrived almost a half an hour early just in case. Just in case what? I had no idea, but I did this all the time, arriving for appointments way before the time as if by doing so everything would turn out better. It never quite worked that way, but I couldn't help it. My dad constantly reminded me that I was always late for everything. "You always delayed me and your mom," he says. "We had to start getting you ready ahead of time to make sure you'd be ready on time."

I spotted Li Qiang's tall body walking in from the early darkness, his eyes roaming the shop, looking for me, I hoped. My heart fluttered as I waved like a fool until he saw me.

"Have you been waiting long?" he asked, sitting across from me, his ever-present brown backpack tossed to the corner of the booth. "I'm not late, am I?"

"No, I came early to read for a while." Shit. I was the worst liar ever; I had no books with me. "I have a great e-book on my phone." *Stop it! Just tell him the truth.* "Sorry, I'm a bit nervous. I have a tendency to be the early bird."

He stretched his arm across the table and covered my hand with his. "Why would you be nervous? This will be fun." That's what I was afraid of; that it would be so much fun I wouldn't want it to end. "It's like being in a play, except the world is your stage." How Shakespearian of him.

A server I had never seen before came to take his order and lingered way longer than she had to, her blue eyes never leaving Li Qiang's. Something began boiling inside of me. The girl was pretty and in her early twenties, I guessed. She was about his age and much more suited for him than me. My cheeks burned—whether in frustration, anger, or embarrassment I couldn't be sure. Maybe a mixture of all of them.

"Is Marcy not here today?" I asked. Marcy was the owner and *very* married. I couldn't remember a single time she hadn't been at the coffee shop.

"It's her date night with hubby. She asked me to cover for her," the girl said, her eyes never leaving Li Qiang who, to his credit, didn't spare her a glance.

The young server finally moved on, but by then I had been fried to a crisp by my own surging blood. In an attempt to hide the weird color I was sure covered my face, I took a big gulp of the coffee and almost choked; the coffee was ice cold. I hated cold coffee. All I wanted to do was spit out my mouthful back into the mug but made myself swallow the whole thing.

"You're okay? Is the coffee too hot?" Li Qiang looked concerned. "You're so red."

Oh boy, awesome. "I'm fine," I said hastily. "So, how are we going to do this?" When everything else fails, divert the conversation.

He let go of my hand, and a sense of longing replaced his warmth. "We'll have to get to know each other well before the show is recorded." Made sense. "We still have a nice buffer between now and that date. I suggest we meet every day after work and talk. What do you think?"

I nodded, nerves catching my voice. "Where do we start?"

"I've been wanting to check out that new restaurant on Main." I knew what place he was talking about; it was a beautiful, small Thai restaurant rumored to serve delicious food. "Unless you don't like Thai food."

"I love Thai," I rushed to say. "I've been meaning to go there too."

That beautiful smile of his erupted again. "Perfect, it's a date." I flinched at his words, thankful he was distracted by the server with his order. He stirred the black coffee—not sure why, there was no sugar—took a sip, and then looked back at me. "We must tell people at work we're dating to make it believable." My heart sank. That was what I was dreading; what was my staff going to think when they were told their boss was dating one of the interns? Who was much younger than she was. "Do you think it will be a problem?"

Might as well tell him the truth. "You are not only my intern but also ten years younger than me. I'm afraid I will be judged big-time."

"Men date younger women all the time," he said, a hint of anger in his voice. "What a double standard. Just let them think what they want. You're the boss, after all." He winked, carving a cute dimple on his right cheek. How come I had never noticed that dimple? "Let's do it tomorrow morning when everyone is in the office, yes?"

I guess it was better to do it early rather than later, so I nodded, resigned to be the topic of gossip for the next month or so. "Sure. Might as well."

Li Qiang chuckled. "You don't look too excited. I'm not a bad boyfriend, I promise." I totally believed that. In the couple months he'd been working for us, he had shown himself to be a true gentleman. He attracted females like a beacon with his good looks, soft voice, and impeccable manners. "We have to come up with a story of how we started dating since it's going to be a surprise for everybody." And a total disappointment for the ladies. "I thought we can tell them we started dating when you went to that conference last month."

"But you didn't go." It had been a weeklong affair in Florida surrounded by a bunch of boring businesspeople. I spent a lot of my time locked up in my room reading.

"I was sick that week," he said, a wicked smile lifting the corners of his lips. "I can say I lied about being sick because I didn't want anyone being suspicious of where I really was. I met you there to let you know how I felt about you, and the rest is history. We waited to tell the staff about our relationship because we wanted to make sure it would work first." He'd given this a lot of thought. Well, he *was* a writer. "What do you think?"

I had to give it to him; his story was straight from a romance novel. I smiled. "Are you sure you're not a romance writer?"

His narrow eyes twinkled with mischief. "I'm sure, but I have read one or two." He studied me for a moment, and my blood started to boil yet again. "You'll be all right," he said in his low, soft voice. "I won't let you down."

I wasn't afraid he'd let me down, but I was afraid I would. Acting was not my forte.

CHAPTER THREE

REVEAL

It had been a sleepless night. Wild dreams kept flipping me around like a pancake all night. When morning came, not even the gallon of coffee I drank before leaving for the office made a dent in my crankiness. I couldn't remember a time when I had been this nervous, other than the one time I auditioned for a dancing part in a high school production. My legs shook, deodorant-challenging sweat gathered under my arms, and specks of light dotted my vision.

Amber Lee was the only person at the office when I got there. She normally opened for me, and I closed. I had a staff of five full-time workers and two interns, plus a few temps who came and went as the need arose. I went straight to the coffee machine, the only fancy thing in my agency, to brew myself yet another cup. I needed all the caffeine I could get.

"What the hell is wrong with you?" My friend gave me a suspicious sideways glance as she shuffled some papers on her desk, the only one other than mine by a window. Outside, morning had not broken yet, and the blinking lights of the old-fashioned theater across the street flooded my office with color.

"I won't tell you," I said. She glared at me, and I added, "I need you to be as surprised—or at least a little surprised—when I break the news to the rest of the staff."

She dropped the papers on the desk and gaped. "Holy shit, you're pregnant." She laughed at her own silly joke. It was my turn to glare at her. "All right, all right. I guess you're announcing your fake relationship today, then."

I sighed and stirred some sweetener into my coffee. "If I don't faint before that. I don't know what I was thinking, Lee Lee."

She scoffed. "You were thinking the boy is hot and how could fake dating him hurt anything?" Not even close, but maybe there *was* a little truth to it. "Relax, girl. You'll be fine."

I turned to her, outraged by her aloofness about the whole mess. "Relax? I'm about to commit fraud—I'm sure there is some law that forbids a businesswoman from lying to the media about her relationships."

Amber Lee resumed her desk cleaning. "Don't be stupid. It's a little white lie that won't hurt anyone and will probably be good for your business."

Dropping to a nearby chair, I humphed. "You know I don't lie. Ever." Yes, I was a goody two-shoes when it came to stuff like that. Lying made me break out in hives. Literally. I hadn't even done it yet and was already feeling the burn under my sleeves. "I hate this."

"Well, not sure how to take that, girlfriend." Li Qiang was either super stealthy or I had been so preoccupied I hadn't noticed him walking in. Had he just called me girlfriend?

"Wait! What? You guys are dating?" Amber Lee's face contorted into what she thought looked like shock.

"Cut the crap, Amber Lee," I said. I turned to my fake boyfriend and tried to smile. "She knows. There's no hiding anything from her." I shrugged, resigned, and he gifted me with another of his amazing smiles. I melted, some of my jitters soothed by the sunshine in his face. "Are you ready?"

He crossed the room to stand by my side. "Present and ready to roll." I wish I was that sure about this whole thing. It was comforting that he was so willing though. If we pulled through this one, I would never be able to thank him enough.

Li Qiang made some coffee for himself, and we all waited for the rest of the staff to arrive. There was a scheduled staff meeting that morning, but little did they know what was about to hit them. Instead of the clients' love life, we would be discussing mine. How lame. How embarrassing.

By nine, everyone had trickled in and settled

themselves at their desks with the donuts I had brought in and the coffee my fake boyfriend brewed for each one of them. If they suspected something fishy, they didn't show it, everyone chitchatting and munching on the sugary treats while they waited for me to take the stage, so to speak.

It was time. Shaking inside, I put on my businesswoman's metaphorical hat and stepped to the middle of the room where everyone could easily see and hear me.

"Good morning, guys. I hope you're enjoying the calories and caffeine." Everyone chuckled while I discreetly wrung the edge of my sweater. "I apologize ahead of time because today's meeting is going to be a little different, and we will need to meet again to discuss our usual agenda." The laughter faded as their eyes trained on me, curious and probing. *I can do this. I can do this.* From the corner of my eye, I saw Li Qiang position himself to be at an arm's length from me when the moment came. "I wanted you all to know this first since it will all be made public soon." I cleared my throat, my eyes unconsciously straying to my so-called boyfriend.

Maybe he could read minds, or maybe he was just really good at reading body language. My hesitation was his cue to step forward, stand beside me, slide an arm around my waist, and face the astonished faces of my employees. "What Ivy is trying to say is that we are dating."

The silence that fell over everything and everyone was not unexpected, but troublesome just the same. People exchanged glances, lips moved without uttering any sounds, and Amber Lee hid her smile behind a hand. Brat! I would have to kill her later. She was enjoying the show.

"Yes, Li Qiang and I started dating when I was at that conference in Florida last month," I continued, encouraged by the discreet tugging at my waist. "Maybe I should have told you all sooner, but we were not sure where this relationship was going and didn't want to make too much of a deal about it." Nobody spoke. I swallowed the sourness on my tongue. "Are you going to be okay with this?"

As suddenly as the silence had descended upon them, the noise returned. If a moment ago I feared angry frowns and sarcastic comments, I got none of that. Instead, my employees jumped out of their seats to come hug me and Li Qiang, congratulating us and wishing us all the best. I was stunned. They actually seemed happy about this.

"We so hoped you two would get together," one of them said, her lips stretched wide in a smile. "We couldn't miss the looks between the two of you. It was so cute." What looks? There had been no looks. Ever. "Li Qiang could never take his eyes away from you." Wait! What? I gawked at my fake boyfriend who had been spirited away from me by a small throng of congratulatory females. He shrugged and smiled sheepishly. Had he really been watching me when I wasn't looking? How come I had never noticed it? What did it all mean?

With my head still reeling from their unexpected reaction, I raised my hand above my head. "Wait, guys, this is not all," I said, my voice a few notches higher than usual. The chatter stopped, and every eye turned to me. "I signed a contract with WATV for our agency to be featured in a news spotlight." Excited whispers made a comeback, but I continued, wanting all of this to be over. "There is a possibility some or all of you will be interviewed. Please, be professional and speak the truth. Our mission should be loud and clear in everything we say. I'm hoping this will result in more clientele."

Amber Lee jumped in. "Who knows? Maybe we'll have to move to a bigger office soon." I really hoped not. I truly loved the location and the space itself of our current office. But if we did have to add more employees to our staff, then we would have to make a move. I was vindicated by a soft grumble of discontent. So I wasn't the only one who loved our little suite. "I'm sure we'll be able to find a bigger but equally great space if we do."

"Thank you for your patience and support. My door is open, as usual, for any questions you may have." Everyone stared as if unsure of what to do next. I shook my hand toward them with my boss smile. "Back to work, people."

Only Li Qiang remained, his eyes still glued to mine. "That went well," he said, his dimple making me warm inside. I nodded, tongue-tied all of a sudden. He crossed the space between us in two strides and kissed my cheek, his lips lingering close to my ear long enough to whisper, "Hi, girlfriend." I giggled like a teenager and covered my mouth to hide it from the staff. It turned out not to be necessary. Everyone was looking at us in cheesy awe, a few *awws* reaching our ears. Heat climbed up my neck and settled on my face again. Li Qiang kissed me again. "I have some errands to run," he said, a twinkle in his eye. "See you later?"

I watched him leave the office, all height and good looks, his usual white shirt stretched taut across the muscles of his back and the seat of his jeans… oh hell, why was I staring at his butt?

CHAPTER FOUR

EATING WITH THE DEVIL

I was in agony. *Not even the expensive and meticulously* applied makeup or the sexy high-heeled boots I was wearing could make me feel better. Inside my head, all I could hear were the words "Dead woman walking." It was always like this when I met my dad for lunch. Thankfully, it only happened about once a month, which was one time too many. I loved him, but there was no one in the world who could make me feel like he did. Not in a good way.

"Stop fidgeting," Amber Lee said, slapping my shoulder playfully. I scowled, misery oozing from every pore in my body. Why couldn't I have Hermione's time-turner necklace? Then I could just be done with this lunch from hell already. My friend sighed. "I could go with you, you know. He won't be able to be as obnoxious if there is a witness." He most definitely could and would. There was no stopping my father's poisonous fumes.

I shook my head. "No, if I brought company, it would just enrage him and make it doubly worse." I licked my lips, took a deep breath, and grabbed my purse. "Might as well get it done."

"I don't know why you put up with his crap," Amber Lee said with a frown. "I know he's your father, but…."

I sometimes didn't understand it either. It was as if he had invisible strings tied to me, like I was a puppet, helpless and totally under his control. Distance always made me question myself. Was it because I loved him? Or was I so weak I didn't have the balls to stand up to him? In my head, I often planned to tell him to shove it next time. Then next time came and those strings, those strangely strong ties, pulled me toward him again. *He's my father. He's just a little rough around the edges. He doesn't mean it.* Except I knew—at least, most of the time—that I was fooling myself and yet didn't seem to be able to do anything about it.

"I'm an idiot," I said, sliding my hands in the sleeves of my coat.

"But a lovable one," my friend said with a chuckle. "Let me kick his ass for you, will you? You'd make me very happy."

I laughed. Amber Lee had known my father since we were both in elementary school, years before my mom died, and her dislike for him had only grown over the years. I didn't think she would ever forget or forgive what my father had done at my mother's funeral. I wasn't sure I could either. I was all for second chances, but that one had been very hard to swallow, and I couldn't be certain I actually did. I brushed those memories away. I needed a clear head to face my father.

"If I did, you'd end up in prison, and then who would be here to tell me how adorable I am?" I chuckled again, my hand closing around the keys. "Time to face the music."

Amber Lee opened my front door. "You mean the monster." She smiled a bit sadly. "Take no prisoners, girl. I'm not kidding; don't let that asshole make you feel less than the fabulous woman you are."

The drive to my father's restaurant of choice, a fancy French place that served tiny, flavorless food that cost a fortune and was also my least favorite in town, was too short. I sat behind the wheel in the parking lot, listening to meditation music, taking calming breaths, and thinking of Li Qiang to take my mind off what the next hour or so would be like. The knowledge that I would be meeting him after this torturous lunch was comforting. God knew I would need his beautiful smile and sexy voice to bring me from the hellish place my visits with my father always threw me into.

My phone buzzed, scaring me out of my paralysis. It was my fake boyfriend. My heart danced a little jig. "Hello?"

"Hey, I was thinking of you and decided to call,"

he said, his voice just as effective at calming me down as any yoga breathing. "Can you talk?"

I nodded, and when I realized he couldn't see me, I added, "Yes, I have a few minutes."

"Where are you?"

I inhaled deeply, debating whether to tell him or not. "I'm sitting in my car outside this stupid restaurant, gathering courage to go meet with my father." He was doing me this major favor, why wouldn't I trust him with this too?

"That bad? What did you do? Hightail it out of the country with his money?"

I chuckled. "I wish. I've never been up to his high standards, and he never wastes an opportunity to remind me of that." Somehow telling him this lessened the weight on my chest and shoulders.

He was silent for a moment. "What the hell did he expect? Wonder Woman? Because you are so fucking awesome, it's hard to imagine him thinking you don't measure up."

My heart liquefied a little, and a stupid smile peeked at me in my rearview mirror. Sweet man. "Nice of you to say that, Li Qiang, but in his book I'm severely lacking. Families, can't live with them, can't live without them." Not true. I'd be perfectly happy living far, far away from my father, but then he'd probably figure out a way to bring cyberbullying to a totally different level.

"Need reinforcements?" Surprised as I was by his

offer, I was also grateful.

"I'll be okay. I have developed a thick skin over the years." But my father's bullets could pierce through armor. I wasn't about to tell him that. The last thing I wanted was for him to feel sorry for me.

"Where are you meeting him?"

"Maison Chic." Even the name of the place was pompous. "I'll be here for about an hour and then come to meet you, if that's okay."

"I can't wait," he said, a smile in his voice. "Try not to choke on the mini-food they serve there."

I was still laughing when I hung up. I was a lot calmer now. Not quite ready to face my father—that would never happen—but the closest I was going to get. I got out of the car, locked it, and walked decisively to the restaurant front door. No prisoners tonight!

♥ ♥ ♥

I'd never understand how a country with such great food inspired such terrible posh restaurants. I had been to France before and never been served the ridiculous fare that hoity-toity so-called French restaurants passed as gourmet food in the US. Not that I could eat much anyway since my stomach was tied up in knots as I sat across from my father, playing target to his game of put-downs.

I anxiously glanced at my watch. I still had another half hour left on the promised hour-long dinner my father had wrangled out of me once I'd finished college. When I looked up, my eyes crashed with the ice of my father's. "Still not able to keep focused on a conversation," he said, a forkful of whatever the green thing on his plate was hanging halfway to his mouth. "How old are you now? Thirty?"

"Almost thirty-six, Dad." My weak protest met with deaf ears.

"How can you ever succeed in life if you can't even pay attention to a simple conversation with your father?" There they were, the bullets, the emotional missiles my father was such an expert at shooting.

I took a deep breath, knowing all too well that what I was about to say wouldn't make a lick of difference. "I *am* successful, Father. I own and run a perfectly thriving business."

His icy blue eyes sharpened as his lips turned into a scowl. "What you run is not a proper business, Ivory Marie." God, I hated when he called me that. "How is matchmaking a real business, a respected one? You might as well be the local *yenta*. God knows you're old enough to be one."

"A *yenta* is not a matchmaker, Dad, just a busybody." Why was I even trying to correct him? It would only make him angrier.

He slammed a fist on the tabletop, and every eye in the restaurant turned to us. He didn't care. "Now you're going to give me Yiddish lessons? You should be more concerned with your life. When are you going to get married? Give me grandchildren? Make me proud?"

I wanted to tell him about the news station and their interest in my business. I wanted to tell him I didn't need a man to be successful and that I would have children if or when I wanted them. Instead, my heart was drowning in its own blood so I hung my head and bit my lip, willing myself not to say a word and hoping time would go faster.

My father pointed at my plate with his knife. "Eat. You're nothing but skin and bones. How will any red-blooded man want you looking like that? And that dress, couldn't you have worn something a little more sophisticated? It looks like a bag." I had worn a cream, boho-style dress that reached a hand width over my knees. The lacy sleeves hugged my biceps and flared from the elbows to my hands. I had paired this soft, feminine outfit with knee-high, brown suede boots. Hardly a bag-looking outfit.

"Hi, sweetheart." I froze. Could it be? I was probably hallucinating out of despair. "Sorry I'm late." The chair next to me scraped the floor, and the next thing I knew, Li Qiang, dressed in an impeccable blue suit, was sitting by me. I looked up and met his beautiful eyes. He mouthed, "Are you okay?"

I didn't have a chance to answer. My father, mouth agape, said, "Who are you?"

Not missing a step, Li Qiang turned to face the man who gave me half of his genes—however reluctantly it seemed—and offered him his hand. My father didn't take it. "I apologize, sir," he said, a friendly grin on his lips. "I'm Li Qiang, Ivy's boyfriend. I was unfortunately delayed at a business lunch. I apologize for the lateness." He then turned to me and covered my hand with his. "How's my sweet *gūniáng*?" I had no idea what he had just called me, but I was not going to let my father know. Li Qiang would tell me later. "I hope you're almost done with lunch because we have to run."

For once, my father looked as if he had lost the power of speech, his hand still holding the fork aloft and mouth ajar. I knew it wouldn't last long, so I had to take this chance to say my goodbyes. "I was about done," I said, making a move to grab my small purse on top of the table. My wonderful, if fake, boyfriend stood up and pulled out the chair for me. "Well, Father, this was… delightful as usual. I guess I'll see you again next month."

Li Qiang smiled at me and then at my father with a slight tip of the head. "Nice to meet you, Mr. Tower. You must be so proud of your daughter. She's not only beautiful but also smart and accomplished." I could have kissed him right then, but instead just smiled like a loon. My father was still struck dumb, so I gently pulled on Li Qiang's hand to rush him. He got the message. "Goodbye, Mr. Tower. Enjoy the rest of the evening." *Or just choke on your expensive wine.* Not a very kind thought, and guilt immediately hit me as always. He could be as obnoxious as he pleased, but I was the one left with the guilt. What was wrong with me?

Only Li Qiang's steady hand kept me from running out of the restaurant after I retrieved my coat from the cloakroom. As soon as the cold air of the day hit my face, I let out a sigh of relief. My pretend boyfriend was not smiling anymore. "Why do you let him talk to you like that?"

I whipped my head up. "You heard what he said?" I hadn't noticed him until he spoke, but now I wondered how long he had been standing there, listening to that wreck of a conversation. Embarrassment heated my cheeks. "How much did you hear?" And why had he come? We were meeting afterward, and I had driven there so there was no reason for him to show up like that. Was he stalking me?

His luscious lips were set in a tight line. "I heard enough to tell your father needs to be taught a lesson about how to treat his daughter." Anger oozed from his words. "Sorry I just showed up like that, but after overhearing Ms. McKenzie's comment yesterday about your father-daughter lunches being emotional torture, I…." He paused, his breathing a bit too fast and shallow. "I don't know what I was thinking I could do, but I just couldn't let you face it alone. Sorry. I know I'm butting in where I shouldn't."

I squeezed his hand still holding mine. "I'm glad you did," I confessed. "Even though it is a bit stalkerish." The distress on his face made me burst out laughing. "I'm joking. I don't think you're a stalker."

A hesitant smile grew on his lips. "Seriously, thank you for plucking me away from that torture."

"Glad I could help. Where shall we go?"

My stomach growled. "Can we go somewhere to eat? Somewhere that serves good food?"

He laughed. "Didn't you just have lunch?" He raised a hand. "Wait, don't tell me. The foo-foo dishes at Maison Chic didn't quite qualify as real food."

I threw my head back, chuckling. "Not even close."

We were still walking down the street, hand in hand as if we had done it a million times before. "I know this amazing Moroccan bistro just around the corner. They serve the best swordfish kabobs in town." That sounded heavenly. I loved seafood but rarely ate it because I was surrounded by red meat carnivores. I nodded enthusiastically, and he pulled me along without another word.

I had never felt the need to be rescued by a man. I had put myself through college and started a whole business without any help, other than Amber Lee's. Being independent and self-sufficient was my pride and joy and call to fame, but I had to admit—however secretly and reluctantly—it felt nice to have someone take care of me for a change.

CHAPTER FIVE

THE SLEEPOVER

Li Qiang loved coffee, a good book, and writing. He was also excellent at charming the pants off most women with only his smile and his dimple. Other than that, I didn't know much about this man who was to be my boyfriend for the next few weeks. I knew he was kind and willing to stick his neck out to help someone in need—present case in point—and that he was so easy to talk to I sometimes forgot we were practically strangers.

"I don't want to push you, but we probably should start getting to know each other better." That was the other thing about him; it often looked as if he could read my mind. It was as if we were both wired the same way. "Tell you what. You come to my place tonight, and I will cook something for you. That way you'll get to see my place, and we'll have time to interrogate each other."

I laughed at his choice of words. He was right, even though the idea of being alone with him in his apartment made me a little nervous. Not that I feared he would try anything, but I was not sure I could be trusted. There was no point in denying it; he was winning me over one smile at a time. When this was over, I might end up with a broken heart, something I definitely did not need now or ever.

I spent the rest of the day staring at my laptop and not seeing anything, my mind wildly moving from one thing to another, what-ifs and why-nots invading my every thought. I promised myself not to change my clothes before going to his place, keep it professional, not giving him any hints about the butterflies that fluttered inside my chest every time he looked at me. This was a business arrangement. I would make sure he'd get fabulous references once his internship was over and use my limited influence to provide him the chance of a great job. It was only fair, right?

By the time I stood in the hallway outside his apartment, I had long caved in. At the last minute, I'd dashed home from work to change into date-appropriate clothes, slipping into a pair of jeans and a stylized flowery peasant top. I freed my hair from the bun I'd worn all day, allowing it to fall onto my shoulders in soft waves, and slid my feet into a pair of boots. A touch of lipstick and a pair of simple earrings finished my outfit. Now I stood paralyzed, wondering whether I had made a mistake—getting dressed like that, coming here, breathing the same air as Li Qiang.

The door suddenly opened and a disheveled Li Qiang appeared, thick, dark eyebrows raised in surprise. "What are you doing out here? Did you knock? I didn't hear anything."

I rushed to lie. "I just got here." Why was his hair all up in spikes and angles? I must have frowned because he chuckled and ran a hand over his hair. "Had a fight with the brush?"

"Dinner kicked my butt," he said, opening the door further and showing me in. "I have a confession to make; I'm no cook. I can barely boil an egg. After almost setting the pot on fire, I ordered out." His dimple made an appearance. "I hope you like pizza."

I grinned and followed him inside the apartment. It was a nice space, full of clean, modern lines. There was no clutter anywhere and no carpets on the wooden floors. "Nice."

"Small, but that's all I need," he said, pointing at a high stool by the bar counter separating the small kitchen from the living room. "And all I can really afford. What you see is pretty much all of it, except from my room and bathroom." The mention of his bedroom made me flush. *You're an idiot, acting like a teenage virgin.* "Drink?" He grabbed a bottle of red wine from the counter behind him and waved it in the air.

I didn't drink often. Or at all, really. But I had, on

occasion, enjoyed a small sampling of a red. "Sure. Just an inch, please."

He turned his back to me to pick a couple of wine glasses and pop the cork from the bottle. I couldn't help but admire the rippling of his muscles under his black T-shirt, half tucked in a pair of dark jeans that hugged his perfect butt. Droplets of sweat gathered at the base of my neck and between my breasts. I knew I looked like a freshly boiled lobster by the time he turned back around to hand me the glass of wine. If he noticed, he never said anything, coming around the counter to sit on the stool beside me. We clinked goblets and took a sip. The wine was smooth and rich, leaving a pleasant burn going down. I closed my eyes for a moment, relishing the feeling and praying I wouldn't make a fool out of myself.

"I'm the oldest of three siblings," he said, his lips stained with wine. "A twenty-year-old sister and a ten-year-old brother." He smiled sheepishly. "Surprise baby. My mom calls him a menopause side effect. A good one, she always says. You?"

"I'm an only child," I started, taking a deep breath. Talking about my family was never something I enjoyed doing. "My mother died when I was a senior in high school. Plane crash. She was an art curator for a big museum in town and was on one of her trips to research and find a piece of art for an exhibition. Her small plane crashed between Paris and a small town in Provence."

Despite my determination to stay cool, my voice caught in my throat. It had been almost nineteen years since my mom's death, but it still tore at my heart every time I thought about it. When the call came, I had been home alone working on a paper for school. My dad was out doing whatever it was he did, mostly staying away from the disappointment that was his daughter. I was the first one to find out, and it nearly killed me. My mother was my anchor, my friend, and the only thing standing between me and my dad's poison.

A soft squeeze of my hand brought me back to the here and now. "You don't have to talk about it if you don't want to," Li Qiang said. "Let's just talk about happy stuff today."

I had to smile at that. Yes, happy was good. We shared information about each other for over an hour, laughing at the disasters—like the time he'd been pantsed by an escalator at a New York hotel or the time I had wiped my face on a rag someone at the office had used to clean a glitter spill—and commiserating about the not-so-funny events in our life. I was pleasantly surprised to find out he shared my passion for dance and some of my favorite authors. I had no family to speak of besides my father; Li Qiang was part of a huge family that spanned several continents. We were both bilingual—I spoke French, he spoke Chinese—with a weird and geeky interest in linguistics. My fake boyfriend was so easy to talk to, I almost forgot we weren't really a couple. I was treading in dangerous waters.

After dinner, Li Qiang suggested we move to the couch in the small living room. My head swam as soon as I set my feet on the ground. "Whoa, did the room move?"

With a chuckle, he came around to support me, a hand under my elbow and the other on my waist. "You don't drink much, do you?"

I stared at my glass and hiccupped. I had drunk way more than my body was used to. Not enough to be drunk, but I was definitely a bit elated. "How many of these did I drink?"

Li Qiang led me gently to the couch. "Only two and only half-full. I'll make you some coffee." He turned to go back to the kitchen, but I held his arm and his gaze. God, I loved his eyes, dark as onyx but warm and full of promise. "You're fine. Just a little boozed."

His smile washed over me like a soothing wave. I relaxed into the throw pillows behind me and blinked my eyes. I'd rest a bit while he brewed the coffee. I fought the need to close my eyes even as the world blurred around the edges, my eyelids heavy as old-fashioned brocade curtains. Going under, going… gone.

Have you ever woken up in a place you don't recognize? You feel confused and a little betrayed by your brain that can't quite place you. That's what happened to me when my eyes finally opened from the wine-induced sleep I had fallen into. I had somehow found my way to a bed, where I was snuggled up against a pillow and covered by a warm, white comforter. Nothing in this room was familiar, from the bedding to the abstract art on the walls to the curtainless windows. Outside it was dark, but the room was infused in a soft glow from two night-lights over the headboard.

"Where am I?" I sat up slowly, my head swimming a bit as I moved. I was still wearing my clothes, but my boots were on the floor, carefully lined up by the nightstand. "What the hell?"

I swung my legs over the side of the bed and stood up, groaning as a dull ache pounded behind my eyes. On bare feet, I tiptoed to the door and cracked it open. Li Qiang's place! I was in my pretend boyfriend's bed. But where was he? I stepped quietly through the open space and looked around. He had tidied up. All the dishes had been washed and were now drying on the rack. A soft growl-like sound made me turn to the couch; Li Qiang was stretched over the sofa, hand behind his head, shirtless and sleeping. I froze. Damn, he was fine! He might be slim but had a strong, muscled chest and shoulders. A throw blanket was draped over his legs and waist, baring his sexy, hairless pecs to my shameless eyes. On cue, heat rose to my face and guilt invaded my mind. Why did I feel like a voyeur? It wasn't as if I had planned this, right? Why would he be sleeping without a shirt? It was like waving a carrot in front of a starved donkey. Not that I was comparing myself to a donkey....

He stirred, and I almost swallowed my tongue. The last thing I wanted was for him to catch me staring at him like that. *I'm almost ten years older than him, pervert!* It's like robbing the cradle. I spun on my heels and retreated to the room. I needed to get out of there. I sat down on the edge of the bed, pulled my boots on, brushed my messy hair with my fingers, grabbed my purse, and left the room, heading to the front door.

"Trying to sneak out of here?" Li Qiang's voice startled me into stone. Shit! I looked like a thief, tiptoeing—or trying to in my noisy heels—toward the door. "Where are you going at two in the morning?"

I chanced a glance at him, grateful for the semidarkness; my cheeks were burning. "I need to go home." Was that even my voice? When had it become so squeaky?

Li Qiang was sitting now, his magnificent upper body still very naked but—much to my relief—bottom half covered in a pair of sweatpants. He yawned and rubbed his eyes. "Stay. It's crazy for you to go home by yourself at this time of night." He smiled, his dimple making me swoon. "Besides, you drank...."

I bristled a little. "I didn't even drink a whole glass of wine." My protest fell flat. It was not how much I drank, but how intoxicated I was, and I had been boozed enough to fall asleep on somebody's couch. "It's been a few hours."

He smiled wider. "Come on, girlfriend, what's the

harm in spending the night in my comfy bed?" He had a point, and yet he was also so wrong.

"What will people at work think if they find out?" I was grasping at straws.

"We're supposed to be dating," he said with exasperating logic. "I think people kind of expect us to spend the night together…." He let the last word hang out, his eyebrows shooting upward.

Of course, he was right. I trusted him to be the perfect gentleman, and it wasn't as if I was that besotted or out of control that I'd forget common sense and jump him in the middle of the night. I sighed, dropping my arms alongside my body. "All right, you win. I'll stay."

My fake boyfriend jumped to his feet and chuckled. "Man, you make it sound as if it's torture. Is my bed really that uncomfortable?"

I fought a stubborn smile. "No, it's very nice, but I hate to put you out. That couch doesn't look that comfortable."

He winked. "I can always share the bed with you." A strangled gasp escaped my lips. He laughed. "Just joking. I have slept on that couch many times when my siblings are visiting." He stared at me while I fought my reluctance to smile. "Come on, I will make you some hot cocoa. *Hǎo*?"

It was my turn to furrow my brow. "What?"

A burst of laughter echoed in the small apartment. "It only means 'okay.' *Hǎo*?"

I did smile then. Who could resist Li Qiang's

dimple and sexy voice? "*Hǎo!*"

Thankfully, he slipped into a shirt on the way to the kitchen, or I would have been too distracted, but the hot chocolate was delicious and the hushed, late-night conversation delightful. I went back to bed an hour later with a stupid smile on my face and a head full of the wonderful man who was posing as my boyfriend. As I drifted off to sleep, I caught myself wishing Li Qiang was indeed my real lover.

CHAPTER SIX

BREAKFAST OF CHAMPIONS

My mouth watered, and a thin thread of saliva drooped down from the corner of my lips. What was that delicious smell? Had I died and gone to restaurant heaven? It smelled as if Julia Child had landed in my kitchen and was preparing a breakfast of champions for the most demanding foodies in the world. Wait! This didn't feel like my bed, and I doubted I even had enough ingredients in my fridge to make such a breakfast. I took a deep sniff, my eyes still stubbornly closed. Maybe Julia brought the materials with her. It could happen.

I bolted upright on the bed. "No, it couldn't happen! Have I gone insane?" A little dazed, I surveyed the room around me only to confirm what my mind had been telling me; I wasn't in my room. I suddenly remembered; I was in Li Qiang's apartment. Shit, I was in his bed—a super comfortable, full-sized linen heaven that smelled like him. I rolled out of the bed with the grace of a hippopotamus and almost landed on my ass. A quick peek at the mirror on the opposite wall confirmed that a family of rats had taken residence in my hair and I was showing clear signs of raccoonish kinship.

Disregarding my boots, I visited the bathroom to get rid of what felt like gallons of liquids and to clean up a bit. Marginally better put together, I followed my nose and ventured out of the room.

"*Nǐ hǎo*, gorgeous." My fake boyfriend was in the small kitchen, a black apron over his sweatpants and a plain black T-shirt, waving at me with a wooden spoon. He looked tasty enough to eat, and a surge of hot, molten waves ran through me and gathered in my lower body. *Chill, woman.* "I hope you're hungry. I made us breakfast."

I took another sniff. "Didn't you tell me you can't cook?" I glided on the balls of my bare feet all the way to the counter and sat on the edge of a stool. "So what's all this?" I may have been dreaming earlier, but the food smelled just as I remembered.

"I can scramble eggs like a pro, and the rest was just delivered from the corner bakery," he announced, returning to stirring the eggs in the pan. "Help yourself."

On the counter, there lay a plethora of tasty treats from fresh, heavenly scented pastries and colorful fruit to a French press full of dark coffee and a pitcher of orange juice. I grabbed a plate and a fork and didn't hesitate. I filled my dish with fruit, one croissant, an almond-covered pastry I didn't recognize but that looked delicious, slathered it all with butter, poured myself a cup of coffee with cream, and then dug in even before Li Qiang had the chance to spoon the eggs onto my plate.

Li Qiang laid the pan down on a kitchen towel and leaned across the counter, laughing. "That's some appetite you got there, *gūniáng*."

My mouth full of buttery croissant, I tried to smile, but I was sure it came across as a silly frown. Once I swallowed the giant mouthful, I told him, "I have a weakness for carbs. And what did you just call me anyway?"

He leaned further, his forearms sliding across the counter, his hands getting dangerously close to mine— or at least the hand I was not using to shovel food into my mouth. "It means girl." Okay, so he did see me as a young female, not an old hag. That's good to know. "Do you think it'd be okay if I ate one?"

Why would he ask me that? Right, I was hogging the plate of pastries. Mortified, I shrieked and pushed it in his direction. "Shit! Sorry, I didn't mean…."

His hand grabbed a roll at the same time his chuckle reached my ears. "Just teasing you. You're too easy."

After a moment of hesitation, I laughed with him. This breakfast was making me giddy with its intimacy and comfort. My heart had filled with feelings I couldn't even name but that were overflowing and seeking someone out. Li Qiang was there, and those tendrils of emotional warmth were heading his way.

"Fuck!" I never cursed like that, but I was beginning to panic. Too many feelings toward someone who would be out of my life soon, someone who was only playing a role. I slid down to my feet, wiped my mouth with a napkin, and headed to the room to fetch my boots. "I have to go. I told Amber Lee I would open today." *Liar, liar, pants on fire.* I needed to get out of there, to break the spell that moment was weaving around my heart and soul. I needed a shot of reality.

When I returned from the room, Li Qiang had an amused smile on his face, that magical dimple making my heart dance and my girly bits heat up. "Why do I get the feeling you're trying to get away from me?" Because I was. I smiled weakly and looked around for my purse. "I don't bite, you know."

I guffawed, my stomach clenched so tightly it hurt. "Don't be silly. I just forgot I needed to be at work early today." Finally locating my bag, I made a victorious swipe for it and headed to the door.

Li Qiang was already there, a hand across the threshold, blocking my exit. "Don't get this wrong, boss," he said, mirth in his voice, "but today is Saturday. We're not open." Gah! Busted. My face burned as if I had gotten too close to the sun, so I tried to hide it with my hand. In vain. His smile told me he was well aware of my discomfort. "You can stay a little longer." He lowered his voice and leaned over just enough that his lips were close to mine. "Stay, please."

Was I reading too much into his request? Oh, God, I was becoming stupider by the second. My heart was going nuts inside my chest, my stomach had been invaded by butterflies, and my mouth was drier than the Sahara. "I have to meet with Amber Lee," I rushed to say. "We have some numbers to crunch." Amber Lee did all the math in the business since I couldn't be trusted with digits, but he didn't know that. At least, I hoped he didn't. "Thank you for a lovely dinner and breakfast." Was that a shade of sorrow that went over his eyes? "And thank you for letting drunk old me stay the night."

He smiled then. "Like you are old at all, Ivy," he said, his fingers brushing my face and lingering there. I could feel his warm breath on my skin, and an earthquake shook me from head to toe. "Why do you put yourself down all the time? You're beautiful, smart, successful… you're truly an amazing woman. Can't you see that?"

I knew I had my strong suits, but I also knew there was big room for improvement. My father had made sure I would never forget that. God knew I'd tried. I'd tried to forget years of brainwashing that my rational side knew to be wrong, but that part of me that still wanted to be daddy's girl could not.

With a weak smile, I pulled his fingers away from my face and held on to them a bit longer than necessary.

"Thank you for saying that, Li Qiang. You're very kind."

He shook his head and made his dimple appear again. With a sidestep, he opened the door to let me through, but before I could, he leaned over once again and kissed my forehead. "I'm not kind. I'm just telling you what I feel."

I'm not quite sure how I made it home, my head stuck in the clouds and all my senses focused on that tiny spot of my forehead where Li Qiang's lips had found their mark.

CHAPTER SEVEN

HIVES

My face was hotter than a ghost pepper. I couldn't believe my ears. "No way. That's impossible." The pretty, however artificial, rep from the TV network was sitting across from me, her lips puckered as if she were about to throw me a kiss. "That's just too personal."

She leaned over and patted my hand as if I were a ten-year-old in need of comforting. "But that's what the public wants," she said in her on-screen voice. "They want to see the real you, the personal side of the woman who leads such a successful love business." I huffed, and she tightened her fingers on my hand. "They want to see that you don't only preach but live it. You know, the old adage, *leading by example*."

"But that's an invasion of privacy, isn't it?" Panic was choking me. "How can I let the whole country see where I live?"

Teresa shook her head, but her perfect curls didn't even budge. "We will make sure there's no clue about where the place is," she assured me with a slight roll of her eyes. "All they will see is the inside of the apartment, not the outside. No markers revealing the location."

I was not convinced. Teresa had shown up at my office that afternoon with a bomb; they wanted to bring cameras to my love nest—her words, not mine. I had no love nest. Hell, I had no lover, and my apartment smelled and looked exactly like what it was: a single woman's house. Not one item in it would even qualify it as a place shared with a male.

"Come on, let's call your boyfriend and see what he says." Teresa's suggestion made my skin itch. "Where is he? He's such a handsome man. You're a lucky devil with such a sweet, young thing wrapped around you."

I'm not going to lie; I blushed furiously and had the strange and compelling urge to strangle the beautiful, too well-put-together woman in front of me. She had noticed the age difference. I had hoped, however foolishly, that I looked young enough that the gap between the two of us wouldn't be too obvious. It looked as if I had been fooling myself.

As if on cue, Li Qiang walked in the office, his lips stretched into the smile that always made my body tingle. He was wearing his usual work pants and white shirt, long sleeves rolled to his elbow and stretched over his well-toned biceps.

"Morning, ladies," he said, striding toward me as if he owned the office. He stopped beside me and brushed his lips on my cheek. "Hello, lovely *gūniáng.*"

The TV rep smiled from ear to ear, her perfect complexion changing to a pale pink. "Morning, Mr. Li. You're looking well." She meant hot. She was practically salivating. *Back up, lady. That's my man.* Wait, no he wasn't. What was I thinking? "We were just talking about interviewing the two of you in your home."

My fake boyfriend threw me a quick glance before replying, "But we haven't moved in together yet." I let out the breath I was holding.

Teresa waved a hand. "It doesn't matter," she said, taking a step closer to him. Before I could stop myself, I intercepted her move and placed myself between the two. How embarrassing. She looked annoyed but kept going, "As a modern couple, I can't believe that you don't spend time in each other's houses, right?"

Li Qiang's laughed. "Ah, the illusion of television," he whispered. Then louder, he added, "I see. Well, we spend most of our time together at my place." I whipped my head up and he smiled. "It's closer to the office." His apartment was indeed just a couple blocks away from the office while mine required driving.

The woman clapped her hands and actually hooted. "So that's settled then. We will come over this weekend and record you in your own love habitat."

I was going to puke and fervently hoped it would go

all over her very expensive shoes. Love habitat? What the hell was wrong with people? Next thing I knew they would be asking to come and film us in our sleep. I hadn't signed up for a reality show. I had signed up for an interview. This was getting totally out of hand.

After she left, I turned to Li Qiang, resolved to tell him I was calling it quits, but he held my hands in his and said, "Don't panic. You've been to my apartment, so you're familiar with it. We'll bring some of your stuff to my place this week and make it look as if you spend a lot of time there." He chuckled. "You've even slept in my bed. So no big deal."

I was beginning to hyperventilate. "But it's such an intrusion in our private lives." My protest was met with more laughter. Maybe I was worrying too much. "This makes me very uncomfortable, Li Qiang." As if to prove it, I pulled one of my hands from his and began scratching my neck.

He tilted his head to the side and then let go of my other hand to touch the skin at my collar. "You're breaking out in hives," he said. "Are you really that nervous?"

I nodded, my neck itching even worse. "I don't like to be the center of attention. I'm not good at it." Or so my father had always told me. *"Girl, don't embarrass yourself and your family. Stay in the background."*

His smile died on his lips. After a moment of silence, he said, "You have to give me a nickname. Calling me by my full name is very formal. Westerners might not notice, but your Asian followers will."

"What can I call you? Do you have a nickname?"

"Some of my friends call me Xiǎoli, but you can call me whatever you want." He said it with a mischievous grin, and I had to fight the urge to smile.

"I like it." I meant it. There was a playful, attractive tone to it that seemed to fit him, even though I had no clue what it meant, if anything. Let's face it, most nicknames are meaningless beyond the emotion we attach to them. My father always called me by my full name, Ivory Marie and my mom called me E because, she said, both my names ended with that sound. I suspected she had never liked my father's choice for my first name, so she made sure to call me something totally different. "Xiǎoli." It rolled off my tongue as if it had always belonged there. "I love it."

"You don't mind me calling you Ivy, do you?" Mind? I loved it. It made me feel special. I shook my head. "Good. So do you want me to come over and help you pick some things up to take to my place?"

Why did that sound and feel so intimate? It wasn't as if we were actually moving in together; it was simply a staging for the sake of the onlooker—which in this case was a damn TV show. "Sure, after work?" He nodded, threw me a cryptic look, smiled, and left the office.

"Xiǎoli," I whispered to myself. With a sigh, I dropped to my chair and settled to go back to work. That's when I noticed my neck no longer itched.

❤ ❤ ❤

Amber Lee was having too much fun, her face twisted into a mask that could be interpreted as much of laughter as of pain. I gave her a dirty look and continued collecting a few books from my shelf. "Not funny, my friend," I snapped at her.

"I beg to differ, Ivory dear," she said, barely controlling her laughter. "You're acting like a virgin bride on the night of your wedding."

I humphed and shoved one book into the bag a bit too roughly. "I am not."

She laughed in response, not trying to even hide it this time. The front doorbell rang, and she jumped to her feet. Before I could stop her, she had run to the door and opened it. "Li Qiang," she exclaimed as if she hadn't just seen him an hour ago at work. "Ready to pick up your bride?"

I would have strangled her if there were no witnesses. With Amber Lee, it was always as if we were back in high school. "Don't mind her," I yelled at them. "She hasn't achieved maturity yet. Come in and help yourself to something to drink." I ran by the store on the way from the office to buy some sodas and a couple cartons of juice. I had seen my so-called boyfriend mix juice with soda on more than one occasion, and I had felt the need to do something nice for him.

Tall and slim, Li Qiang dropped his bag on the floor and sat on the arm of the couch. "Thanks, Ivy," he said, that wicked dimple back for an encore. "Are you about done?"

I had been collecting items from the house that I thought would be things I would take with me to the house of a SO; there were some books, a special blanket, a pillow, some food items, a puzzle I hadn't been able to crack in the almost two years since I bought it. I also packed the two copies of Li Qiang's books he had given me at my request. I was almost finished with the first. I showed the bag to him. "Can you think of anything else?"

He cleared his throat, threw a glance at my friend, and said, "I'm flattered you didn't forget my books, but what about clothing? Underwear, maybe a piece of lingerie or two...." Holy mother of God, my face caught on fire. How had I not thought of that? Why had I left it open to be brought up by no other than him? "Maybe a toothbrush and some toiletries."

I turned away abruptly and almost ran to the bathroom under the pretense of collecting those items, but instead I ran the cold water and splashed my face several times to cool off. Then I picked a toothbrush and a few toiletries and went back to the living room.

"Can you add that to the bag, Amber Lee?" I handed them to my friend and then went back to the room to pick some clothing. I was ashamed to admit I had no lingerie. All my underwear was comfortable and practical, but I still tried to pick those pieces that could be considered sexy and threw them in a bag. *You're not wearing them, fool. Just staging.* I was beginning to hate that word.

We left shortly after, Amber Lee trailing us all the way to my car where she stood to watch us drive away. "Don't do anything I wouldn't do," she yelled out with a mighty wave. I waved back and hid my discomfort with a smile while maneuvering the car out of the parking spot.

Li Qiang didn't own a car, he'd told me. He called himself a public transportation ninja, a rush-hour warrior. "I don't go very far from home anyway, so I don't need a car."

"What if you need to go somewhere you can't take a bus?" I'd ask him. I couldn't imagine not having a car to drive myself around.

"I'll take an Uber," he'd said, shrugging. "Or if I really need to, I'll rent a car." It made sense, I guess. But how many young, professional guys were there in the US without a car?

We parked in the building's underground parking lot and then took the elevator up to the third floor where he lived. His apartment felt strangely familiar, considering I had only been there once before.

Li Qiang had emptied a couple drawers in his dresser and made some space for my clothes in his closet. He showed me where everything was and then left me to go make coffee. I suspected he knew how uncomfortable this was for me and didn't want to make it harder by watching me fold my underwear and place it where his were just a few hours before.

By the time I returned to the living room, he handed me a steaming cup of coffee. The mug had a big, dark pink heart printed on it and the wording Love Conquers All. "I didn't picture you for the type to buy this kind of mug," I told him, dropping to the seat beside him on the couch.

He laughed. "I'm not. I bought it for you to keep here." Leaning in, he licked his lips, eyes bright with mischief. "Do you like it?"

Lightheaded, I swallowed my discomfort and nodded a bit too emphatically. "I do, it's very cute." And very me. How did he know?

After a brief moment of silence, Li Qiang leaned back on the couch, crossed one leg over the other knee, and took a long gulp of coffee. "When is the TV person doing the interview?"

I sighed, happy to move the attention away from me. "This weekend sometime," I said vaguely. Teresa had not been too specific. "Maybe I should call and ask her when exactly." I pulled the phone out of my pocket and punched in the number she had given me. She answered right away. "Teresa, this is Ivory Tower. Sorry to bother you, but I needed to know when you're planning on coming for the interview."

"Hi Ms. Tower, no bother at all." Her TV voice came across distant but perky as usual. "We actually decided not to give you a specific day or time so it will be more natural, but it will be in the next couple weeks. We want to make it organic, you know."

The very unlike-me words *what-the-fuck* crowded my thoughts, and I caught myself opening and closing my mouth soundlessly, much like a fish tank treasure chest. Li Qiang opened his eyes wide, thick eyebrows rising. I shook my head, still unable to articulate a coherent thought. "But, but…." Yeah, not one intelligible thing.

"I can tell you it will be sometime in the evening, after five most likely." Teresa said it with such authority there wasn't any room for discussion. "Don't you worry; just do what the two of you always do, and we'll just crash the party." She giggled at her own joke. "I'll be in touch." And she hung up.

Paralyzed, I went over her last words. Do what we always do? That would mean each one of us in our own place, nowhere near each other. I was pretty sure that's not what she meant. "Oh, shit! This can't be happening."

My fake boyfriend's expression fluctuated between curiosity and worry. "What? What's wrong?"

It took me a while, but I was finally able to put my scattered and panicky thoughts into words that someone else could understand. My partner in crime seemed a bit shell-shocked too, his eyes stuck in an unnatural round shape as he processed the information. "Xiǎoli?"

My use of his nickname seemed to snap him out of whatever trance he was in. He licked his lips, his eyes going back to their narrower shape. "Well, nothing we can't deal with, right?"

I had no idea what he was talking about. "But if we don't know when they're coming, how can we make sure I'm over here at that time?" I rubbed the back of my neck, a dull headache beginning to pound my brain. "Maybe I can convince her to give us a call when she's on her way here." Even though I doubted she would agree. She seemed determined to be *organic*, whatever that meant. In the words of Inigo Montoya of *Princess Bride* fame, I didn't think that word meant what she thought it meant.

Sudden heat on my forearm made me look up. Li Qiang had closed a hand around my arm. "Calm down. No big deal," he said. Was he nuts? "It's easy. You'll just have to move in for a while."

My butt slipped off the edge of the seat where I had been perching through the whole conversation, and I had to brace myself not to fall off completely. He reached out to support me. "What d-did you just say?"

He smiled then, that sexy dimple winking at me. "You can stay here until they come. I believe you're acquainted with my bed."

Wicked, wicked man. Like that would be the solution and not a gross exacerbation of all my problems. Inconceivable!

CHAPTER EIGHT

MOVING IN

"But why?" I knew I sounded like a child, but this situation was bringing out the worst in me. "Why do I have to move in with someone I barely know just to please the stupid network?"

Amber Lee looped her arm through mine and pushed me gently toward the window in the office. "Honey, this is for your company, your career," she said in the same hushed tones people used to soothe young kids. "And Li Qiang is hardly a stranger. I mean, you've slept together—"

I stopped abruptly and yanked my arm from her. Fuming, I burned her to a crisp with my fiery glance. "We did *not* sleep together." I enunciated each word Professor Higgins's style. "We slept under the same roof. There is a gargantuan difference."

She dismissed me with a wave of the hand.

"Semantics." I huffed and crossed my arms. "The point is, he's not a total stranger, and you couldn't have found more of a gentleman than he is." That was true. The man was respectful and every inch a gentleman, however young. "And I think the real issue here is that one, you are scared to death the studio finds out your relationship is a sham because you're a goody two-shoes who never lies, and two…" She paused, the corner of her lips curling into a know-it-all smile. "The thing is you are so attracted to Li Qiang, you're scared of what may happen if you're alone together for a few days."

Shit. She may not be completely right, but she wasn't completely wrong either. I *was* attracted to Xiǎoli. A lot. I hadn't had a romantic relationship in a while, and romantic fool that I was, I knew I was vulnerable to someone like him: gentle, generous, and gentlemanly. The three Gs—well, four Gs because as much as I would vehemently deny its impact, he was also drop-dead gorgeous.

My friend stepped closer to me again and cupped my elbow with her hand. "Can you please just have fun? Let it go. Be a young woman in your prime and enjoy the ride." I was hardly young, and I had too many responsibilities to enjoy such a caper. Not to mention the very real possibility of my father finding out the truth about this. I would never hear the end of it. "Come on, Ivory Bee, enjoy the fun." The use of my old nickname made me smile. I couldn't remember the last time she had called me that. She had come up with it when we were teenagers, and she thought it was unfair she had two first names and I had only one. She pointed at my face with one long, sharp, scarlet nail. "Aha! I saw that. You're smiling." I shook my head but couldn't hold the chuckle anymore. "See? I knew you still remembered how to laugh."

"Ms. Tower." Marianne ambled over in her high heels, a small notepad in her hand. "Li Qiang called and asked me to tell you he'll go over to your place straight from his meeting with our client at seven tonight to help you with your stuff."

Instinctively I tried to hush her with a gesture of my hand. I didn't want the whole office to know I was moving in with him. "This is not public knowledge, Marianne. Can you keep it down?" I skimmed the area around us and was relieved to find everyone busy with their work. I looked back at her. "I don't like to bring my personal life to work." *You're so full of shit, Ivory.* My inner critic was having a field day.

Marianne made a duck face, pushed her glasses higher on her nose, and walked away. I turned to Amber Lee who was standing behind me, her arms crossed tightly over her generous bosom and an amused twist to her lips. "They know you're dating, so it really wouldn't be that big of a deal for them to find out you're moving in."

I shrugged, feigning disinterest. "Next thing you know, they will be buying me housewarming gifts." I exhaled deeply. There was a heavy tightness gathering in my chest. "I hate that I am tricking them. It's not right."

My friend burst out laughing and walked away, throwing her last words over her shoulder, "You could always make it a reality, you know. Just kiss the guy."

I walked around for the rest of the day with *The Little Mermaid* song, "Kiss the Girl," swimming around in my head.

True to his word, my fake boyfriend was at my door at seven on the dot. He wore a charming smile on his full lips, and his eyes narrowed almost to a slit. What was he so happy about? I was a nervous wreck. I had dropped my suitcase twice on the way to my front door and tripped over the bathroom rug three times. I couldn't stop shaking and hated myself for it. *It's not as if I'm moving in for good.* Yeah, easy to say, harder to swallow.

Li Qiang took the suitcase out of my hands, grabbed the canvas bag I had slung over my shoulder, and walked out. I started to follow but stopped. "Wait, I forgot something." I ran back to the kitchen where I had filled a bag with my favorite treats and a small surprise for Xiǎoli. "Right, I think I got everything."

Soon we were at his place. After taking the bags to the room, I took out the small but sinful chocolate cake I had bought as a thank you for Li Qiang. I knew he was as chocolate crazy as I was; his desk drawers at work were jam-packed with chocolate bars and other chocolaty goodies—not that I had been nosing around in his desk. Delight twinkled in his eyes. "For me?"

I nodded, unable to hold back the smile his joy teased out of me. "A small thank-you for doing this crazy thing to help me." Crazy was an understatement. "I will never be able to thank you enough."

He guffawed, turned on his heels, and opened the kitchen cabinet over the coffee machine. "This is a great start," he said, pulling a couple of small plates out and handing them to me. He opened a drawer and shuffled things around until he found a cake knife. "There are spoons and forks in that basket."

We sat, each on an opposite side of the kitchen bar, forks in hand, and attacked the cake with the enthusiasm of the long starved. After a few bites, I caught him watching me, his fork halfway up to his mouth, bits of the cake falling from it onto the plate below. I stopped my passionate fork action and looked at him, licking my lips clean.

He pointed at the corner of my mouth, a mixture of fascination and amusement in his smile. "You've got chocolate on your face."

For a moment, my rom-com deluded mind thought—hoped—he would reach out and brush the crumbs from my face. He didn't. Li Qiang was too much of a gentleman, and this was real life, not a Hallmark romance. I blushed as the absurdity of my thoughts sank in and rushed to wipe my face with a napkin, giggling awkwardly.

"You're beautiful." The unexpected compliment struck me dumb. His smile had been replaced with an expression I couldn't interpret. I wiped my mouth again for lack of anything better to do, but when I raised my eyes back to him, the expression was still there. "You're not very good at accepting compliments, are you?"

He got that right. I never felt I deserved them, that people were just being kind. "I never know what to say," I confessed, dropping the napkin on the counter and leaning on my elbows.

Another smile stretched his lips. "You don't have to say anything," he said, cutting another slice of cake for himself. "I just wanted to tell you what I think. I think you're beautiful with your long, chestnut hair and twinkling brown eyes." He took a huge bite of the cake, groaned with pleasure, and then continued. "You're also smart, creative, and kind. Oh yeah, and you have the best taste in baked goods."

It was more like a flaw; my love for carbs was nothing to brag about, or so my father always told me—or anyone who was listening. *"One day you'll be as fat as a cow, and then you will remember what I told you about eating all those carbohydrates,"* he had said more than once.

I stood up, wanting to wipe away any memories of my father's thoughtless comments. "Want some more coffee? I can make a killer cappuccino." He nodded, and I strode around the counter to the inside of the kitchen where his fancy espresso machine awaited. He had a beautiful collection of mugs of all sizes and shapes. I noticed the one he had bought for me among them, and a wave of heat ran through me. I busied myself with the coffee, pretending I didn't feel his eyes focused on me, the thrill shooting up my spine and down again until my toes were literally curling inside my shoes. If he could do that to me with a casual glance, I could only imagine….

No, you are not imagining that.

I tried to think of something disgusting to move my thoughts from dangerous territory, but it was useless. My senses were full of Li Qiang. I could smell his subtle lemon verbena cologne, feel the heat of his dark eyes on my skin just as real as if he was touching me, and I could hear his breathing, a little faster than usual, matching the rhythm of mine.

"That smells good." I had been so focused on not obsessing about him that I did not notice Li Qiang approaching and peeking over my shoulder, his mouth so close to my ear I had to fight the urge to lean in. "I'm impressed."

Flustered, I turned around so fast with his cappuccino cradled in my two hands that I almost spilled it all over his immaculate white shirt. "Sorry, I don't know what's wrong with me lately." My body, inside and out, was alive, tingling, and my breath kept speeding up. "I should go and unpack."

He took the mug from my shaking hand and said,

"Come on, I'll help you."

Right, because unpacking my clothes with a hot and sweet number like my pretend boyfriend in the intimacy of his room would be just what I needed at that moment.

I was in so much trouble.

I was in church, which was weird because I hadn't been to church for over a year. But I could hear bells, beautiful vibrating bells that made my body shake and my soul sing. My eyes popped open, and I sat straight up in bed. I was in bed, not at church. Had I been dreaming? Another bell resonated through the house, and my muscles responded immediately by relaxing. Where were the bell sounds coming from? There was no church in the neighborhood that I knew of. I slipped out of bed and into my slippers, these cute furry creatures my awesome boyfriend had bought me.

I padded my way to the main area of the apartment, the sound of the bells louder the closer I got. Li Qiang was sitting cross-legged on the wood floor, eyes closed and hands draped loosely over his knees in deep meditation. The sound of bells and wind chimes came from his sound system and permeated the air like a billowing cloud of peace. I leaned against the side of the doorway, crossed my arms, and watched him in silence. He looked so peaceful, so relaxed, and so damned sexy. He had on a pair of black joggers and a plain white T-shirt, his silky black hair still wet from the shower. My heart sped up, and my skin heated and tingled. Parts of my body came alive.

Shit. Not the time.

I turned around, deciding to take a very cold shower when I heard him call me. "Ivy, wait. I have breakfast ready."

I should have pretended I didn't hear him and kept going, but I couldn't. With each passing day under the same roof, I was getting more and more attached to that beautiful, gentle man. It had been only three days, but it felt like years. We had both fallen into a familiar routine that both pleased and terrified me. This situation shouldn't feel this comfortable, this normal.

"What did you make today?" I asked, backtracking to the kitchen. He had jumped to his feet much like a cat and beat me there by a few seconds. "I smell cinnamon and maybe…" I sniffed the air a couple times. "Maple syrup?"

Li Qiang chuckled. "Oatmeal. You've got a good nose. I added both cinnamon and maple." He spooned the thick, aromatic goo into two bowls and slid one on the counter in front of me. "There are walnuts and pecans in that bowl. I'll get the strawberries."

He turned around to open the fridge, and I—to my utter mortification—checked out his lovely butt. "For someone who can't cook, you sure cook a lot."

Coming back to sit next to me, Li Qiang handed

me a small bowl full of sliced strawberries. "I can do very basic stuff," he said. "My mom would kill me if I hadn't learned. In my house growing up, we all had assigned days to cook breakfast and simple dinners. She cooked for us all week, so on weekends we were expected to give her a break." I liked his mother already. "Which brings me to what I need to tell you." Uh-oh. "My family wants to meet you."

My jaw fell. I was certain I would have swallowed a fly if one happened to go by. "What? Why?"

His hand covered mine on the counter. "Why, because you're my fiancée."

I choked on the spoonful of oatmeal I had just put in my mouth. "Fiancée?" I sputtered, not sure whether to swallow or spit the cereal out. "When did we get engaged?"

To his credit, Li Qiang looked contrite. "Sorry, I should have told you earlier. My parents are very traditional about certain things, and they would have had a fit if they knew we are staying together with no commitment."

"So you told them we are *engaged*? They don't know our relationship is a sham?" I may have shrieked. "Why didn't you tell them the truth?"

He shrugged. "I couldn't, could I? This way if the TV people interview them, they will not have to lie."

Irritation swelled in my chest. "You got to be shitting me! That's why you didn't tell them?" Yeah, I was definitely shrieking now. "That's ridiculous.

You're lying to your own parents so they don't have to lie to strangers?" It didn't sound like him at all, and somehow that irritated me even more. "What are you going to tell them when we're finished with this? That we broke up?"

He nodded first and then shook his head. "Well, I'm kind of hoping I won't have to."

His words made no sense to me at all. "What the hell do you mean by that, Li Qiang? Have you lost your mind completely?"

There was a smile struggling with a frown on his lips as he stood up and held me by the shoulders. For a moment I thought he was going to slap me—you know, the way they do in the movies when someone is hysterical; I *was* slightly agitated.

"Calm down. Let's go sit outside on the balcony." With infinite patience, he steered me to the sliding-glass door that led to the small balcony on the opposite side of the kitchen. Outside, the air was crisp, but the sun was shining. Li Qiang's outdoor space was small but beautiful. There was a fitted bench against the wall on one end of the rectangular space, a bistro table against the half wall, and a small collection of brilliant green potted plants on the other end. Still holding my hand, he sat beside me on the blue, pillow-covered seat. Being with him like this was becoming alarmingly comfortable and familiar. What would happen once we ended this charade? I knew exactly what would happen; my heart would be broken just as effectively as if Li Qiang himself had done the breaking.

"I should have asked you first," he said, his expressive eyes searching mine. "*Duìbùqǐ*, Ivy, I'm sorry." I was inordinately excited that I was beginning to understand some of his Chinese expressions, but on the other hand it made me even more anxious that I was getting that close to him. "I know my parents, and I thought this would be the best way to handle this."

I still was not ready to accept that as a reasonable enough way of dealing with this mess. "They will hate me when it's over," I said, my tone a bit too close to a whine for my liking. "I'll be the entitled white woman who's good for nothing in their eyes after we break it off." I was fully aware of how immature I sounded, but for some reason being liked by his parents—whom I had never met—had become something very high up on my priority list.

Li Qiang laughed softly, patting my hand. "They won't. They'll love you just the same." Which was ridiculous, considering they didn't even know me yet. What if they took a total dislike for me? "They know that any woman who puts up with their son for any period of time is someone they admire."

A burst of laughter escaped my lips. "Why is that? You are—" I was going to say "perfect" but bit my tongue and said, "a good man. You're a good man. Why would they think that?"

"You haven't known me long enough, boss." I confess, every time he used the word boss when addressing me, it made me feel all hot and bothered. I guess there was some truth to the old myth that forbidden love is sexy. "Before we moved here from upper New York, I was well known in my small town as a player."

I snorted. "Stop it! You, a womanizer?" No way. There was no way in hell that sweet, gorgeous man had ever been what he claimed he was. "I can believe you had many girls after you, but womanizer? Come on!"

He raised his hands, palms forward. "All true. Ask my mother when you meet her." Could it really be true? "Well, at least what my family considers to be a Don Juan." He chuckled. "Did I mention my family can be a bit… traditional at times?" What did that mean? "Like still hanging on to some pretty old-fashioned Chinese ideas. My mom and dad are a weird mixture of the modern and old world."

Panic rose in my throat. "More the reason not to tell them we're really dating."

"Trust me." Oh, I hated when people said that. It never boded well. Never. "I know what I'm doing."

I truly hoped so. Nothing made me more uncomfortable than the thought of people hating me. It was bad enough my father did, no matter how hard I tried to change that. I'd resigned myself to the fact that nothing I could do would make my father like me, but hell if I wasn't going to give it all I had with everyone else.

CHAPTER NINE

PLOT TWIST

If I combed my hair one more time, I'm certain it would start talking back at me. I had brushed, twisted, pinned, unpinned, pinned again, twisted some more, and then restarted the whole process over at least five times. I sprayed it with the leave-in conditioner to tame down the static my overzealous combing had caused. With each stroke of the brush, I looked more and more like Albert Einstein, minus the brain power.

"You're making me nervous, and I won't even be here for the whole fiasco." Amber Lee had come over before heading to her manicure appointment. Normally I would go with her and treat myself to a pedicure, but today was the day my fake in-laws were coming to meet me.

Li Qiang was insufferably calm and had offered to grab some Italian for lunch, a suggestion that made me twitch my nose. "Italian? Really? Didn't you tell me your mother is all about healthy food?" I had told him. He simply shrugged and commented that his mom knew he couldn't cook to save his life and that Italian had always been the go-to meal when they wanted to treat the parents. "You can't be pissed off with a bellyful of pasta." Maybe there was some warped truth to that, but I couldn't stomach anything with tomato sauce or anything else acidic. My nervous stomach was already in crisis, so we settled on Greek instead.

"Where the fuck is your lover boy?" Amber Lee asked, her eyes roaming every corner of the apartment. "You'd think he'd be here supporting his girlfriend." Sarcasm peeked from behind her words.

"He went to pick up food at that Greek restaurant down the block," I replied, giving up on the stray hairs that wouldn't be tamed and tied the rest of the rat's nest into a true-to-its-name messy bun. "I figure hummus and roasted veggies would probably go easier on my ulcer and be sophisticated enough for visitors."

Amber Lee snorted. "You don't have an ulcer." She dropped her wide hips onto the edge of the bed and leaned back on her arms. "You love making yourself sound older than you are, don't you?"

It was my turn to snort laugh. "If I don't have an ulcer, I'm sure to end up with one at the end of this craziness, that's for sure." I leaned closer to the mirror to check the state of my mascara and, satisfied with it, turned around to face my friend. "How do I look?"

A twist of her lips, a narrowing of her eyes, and Amber Lee leaned forward, smiled and said, "Not bad for a hundred-year-old woman." I stuck my tongue out at her, and she flipped me the finger, making me laugh. She got to her feet and stepped up closer to me. "You, baby girl, look gorgeous. Li Qiang is the luckiest fake boyfriend in the world. His parents are going to love you and insist you guys get married soon."

I gave her a playful push and humphed. "Stop it. Not funny, Amber Lee. It would be better if they didn't like me. Then I could feel less guilty when we break up."

"Ivory Bee, everything is going to work out just fine." Amber Lee placed both hands on my shoulders and bent down a bit so her eyes were leveled with mine. "Relax. Now I got to go have my nails done. We'll talk afterward." She dropped her hands and stepped out of the room before turning around one last time. "And you have a booger hanging on your nose." I turned around to the mirror in a panic, and I heard her laughing. "Sucker! Relax, woman. Have fun."

I was going to kill her one of these days. She was lucky I loved her so much. I heard the front door opening and closing and Li Qiang's voice mixing with Amber Lee's before it all went silent. I stepped out of the room to find him unloading a few bags of food on the kitchen counter. He stopped and turned to me, his narrow eyes rounding as he scanned me from head to toe. I had put on a two-layer, long dress, the bottom white layer stretching all the way to my ankles, while the top blue one draped over it in asymmetric angles to just below my knees. I loved the dress because it was comfortable and yet feminine, flowing seamlessly over my body.

"You look beautiful." His voice was husky, and his eyes had latched on to mine. Self-conscious, I played with the large crescent-moon pendant hanging over my chest. "My mom is going to love you." That was kind of what I was afraid of. Even though at the same time I didn't want her to hate me. *Shit. Why do I have this need to be liked by everybody?*

"What did you get?" I asked, welcoming the distraction. Li Qiang seemed to snap out of his trance and started pulling containers out of the bags to show me. "We better put that in actual glass dishes, don't you think?"

For the next thirty minutes, we set the table together, arranged the Greek dishes in the surprisingly beautiful casseroles and platters my boyfriend had stored in his cabinets, put the wildflowers he had brought with him in a vase at the center of the table, and just as we took an exhale of relief, the doorbell rang.

Ten-year-old Li Wei was the first one in, bursting through like a ball of energy and throwing himself at his brother in a great bear hug, followed by a series of punches and punts. *Boys!* Li Qiang's mother came in, closely followed by her husband and her twenty-year-old daughter. They all smiled at me as they took off their shoes beside the door. I realized belatedly—like several days too late—that I never thought of taking my shoes off while in the house. Irrational anger rose in my chest toward myself and maybe a little toward Li Qiang who had never told me I should have done it. Another screwup on my part.

With cheeks blazing, I offered my hand to my fake mother-in-law to be, hoping she wouldn't notice I was wearing outside shoes instead of the slippers the whole family had fished out of a small cabinet by the door and now wore. "So nice to meet you, Mrs. Li." A frog had settled in my throat.

Mrs. Li smiled even wider and held my hand within hers. "Sweetheart, Qiang'er didn't lie; you *are* beautiful." Her words only fanned the fire under my skin. "And please call me by my first name, Yue Yan. Mrs. Li is my mother-in-law," she whispered the last words behind her hand and threw an amused glance at her husband who was still struggling with his slippers. "Bao, isn't she a doll?" Li Qiang's dad looked up at me and grinned. "My son is so lucky to have found you."

Was it possible to feel happy and distraught at the same time? When Li Qiang passed close to me, herding his family toward the dining table, I whispered, "Why didn't you tell me not to wear shoes in the house?"

He smiled and whispered back, "This is your house now too. Why would I tell you what you can and can't do? I want you to feel at home, not like a guest." Something inside of me melted. He was perfect, the perfect man for me with one major exception—he was ten years younger than me and just starting his professional career.

It turns out that a meal with a ten-year-old super-active boy makes something that could potentially be an awkward event turn into a perfectly comfortable and informal one. Li Wei didn't get off his seat—thanks to a death stare from his mother—but wouldn't stop talking; from manga to video games to Oreos-eating competitions in school to who could spit the farthest, nothing seemed to be off-limits for him. Relief flooded me, and I made a mental note to buy him some treat as a thank-you. Yue Yan was so busy trying to quiet her son before he made any inappropriate comments that she had no chance at real conversation for most of the meal, and it wasn't until the young boy was sent to the balcony with a tablet and headphones that silence fell upon all of us.

The scraps of leftover food on my plate became overwhelmingly interesting all of a sudden, but even then, I couldn't miss an exchange of glances between Mamma Yue Yan and her daughter. I braced myself for what was coming. "Qiang'er, have you thought about maybe setting the date for the wedding?" That was fast. Apparently, Mrs. Li didn't believe in a long engagement and was not afraid to say so. "It will take time to set up both a traditional and Western wedding, so we must know way ahead of time." All righty then.

My eyes flew to Li Qiang, who seemed amused

rather than terrified like I was. "*Mā*, we just got engaged. Can you please wait a bit before starting to plan the ceremony?" I tried to swallow but couldn't; my throat had gone desert dry. "We need to get used to the idea first."

Yue Yan turned her gaze to me. "Ivory, can you please explain to my clueless son how important it is to plan these once-in-a-lifetime events in plenty of time?" My eyes were bouncing like ping-pong balls from my fake boyfriend to my fake future mother-in-law. What could I say? I had gone from girlfriend to fiancée quicker than lightening.

"Will you stop harassing the poor girl, Yue Yan?" Surprisingly, it was Li Qiang's father who stopped the madness. He wiped his lips with a napkin and smiled at me. "I apologize for my overbearing spouse. She can't wait to plan a wedding now that her best friend's son has gotten married. It's always been a competition between them. Freddy and Li Qiang are the same age and grew up together."

The Li matron humphed, crossing her arms over her chest. "You make me sound like a shallow old woman, Bao. I just want to make sure these two get a perfect wedding."

I finally found my voice and, leaning over slightly, placed my hand over hers. "When the time comes, Mrs. Li, I promise I will come to you. I don't have a mother, and I would be honored to have you in her place." Her smile told me I had said the right thing. "In the meantime, what about a nice cup of coffee?"

Li Fang, my would-be future sister-in-law, stood up. "I will help you, Ivory," she said, placing her napkin carefully on the table. "Tea for my mom and coffee for everybody else." She followed me to the kitchen and began collecting cups from the cabinet onto a tray while I started the brewing. "You're in so much trouble now, girl." Her whisper froze me. Only my eyes could move. "Now that she knows you are motherless, she'll take it upon herself to fill that void in your life." I blinked a couple times. "Congratulations, you just earned yourself an intense—however well-intended—surrogate mother."

Oh shit!

The sun tickled my nose, and the book I had in my hand fell to the padded seat. Had I drifted off to sleep? It was so comfortable on the balcony, the warm sun shining down partially on me, a gentle breeze caressing the skin of my exposed arms. Tomorrow it would be back to work after the long holiday weekend, so I wanted to soak in as many Ds as I could. Li Qiang had gone out to see his family after a call from his mom. We had just seen them the day before at lunch, so I couldn't imagine what might have possibly happened in between to warrant a mad dash to their house. Yue Yan most likely wanted to grill her son about the wedding again. I closed my eyes, lulled by the serenity around me. With the weather as nice as it was, most people were probably out enjoying outdoorsy things, but I enjoyed a more indoor outdoors.

"Ivy?" Li Qiang was back. I straightened and called to him. In a blink, he opened the sliding door and stuck his head outside. "There you are." He stepped over the small ledge and closed the door behind him. "It's beautiful today, isn't it?"

I nodded and patted the seat beside me. "Come enjoy it with me." He sat down next to me, leaned back until his head hit the back wall, and sighed with his eyes closed. "What happened? Is everything okay?"

He opened one eye only, his lips pulled comically up the opposite side. "Promise me you won't kill me and throw me over the balcony."

I guffawed and slapped his upper arm playfully. "Stop messing around. What's wrong?"

Straightening on his seat, my beautiful fake boyfriend hesitated for a moment before saying, "Wei're has chickenpox." That was strange. We had talked about that the day before. Li Qiang's mother seemed to have been very interested in knowing whether I had chickenpox as a child. Coincidence? "My father has never had it so—"

"No!" I could guess what was coming next as clearly as if I could read his mind. "No, it can't be."

He hung his head. "Sorry. She knows you've had it and I had it, so she wants my brother to stay with us during the infectious stage." He turned his head to look at me. "I'm sorry. I know she's making this up. Li Fang told me Mom was awfully suspicious when she saw a pile of bed linen folded under the cocktail table yesterday." Shit. Had we left it there? "Now she wants a spy to make sure we're actually together."

"I thought she was traditional and would be happy if we weren't sleeping together."

He shrugged off another sigh. "You would think, right? But she is my mom, a very complicated mixing pot of cultural and personal beliefs. She doesn't believe that a full-blood American like you would not sleep with her fiancé."

I was not sure how to react to that. "I feel I should be offended," I said, not offended at all. "When is he coming?"

"Tonight. He'll be sleeping on the couch." Which meant Li Qiang would have to move in the room with me. It was a very small room with barely any floor space for his six-foot-plus frame. I must not have hidden my horror too well because Li Qiang's smile broadened. "Don't look so terrified. I promise I won't bite."

I opened and closed my mouth a few times, fish out of water that I was, and managed to stutter out, "B-But, we-we'll ha-have to sl-sleep together."

He laughed in earnest now. "Not together, just in the same room," he said, when he was able to stop his laughter for a few seconds. "You worry too much, Ivy." I didn't worry enough. If I had worried like I should have, I wouldn't be in this position right now.

Li Qiang didn't waste any time; he washed linens, set a blanket and a pillow out for his brother, and hid a set for himself under the bed. As a courtesy to me, he had been taking showers in the tiny guest bathroom in the living room, so we had to move his toiletries back to the main bathroom. I'll admit, the business of setting up for his brother's stay kept me away from thinking too much about what was going to happen when it was time to go to bed later that night.

Li Wei showed up at the door with a small duffel bag and a laptop. "He has his earbuds in the bag," Li Fang said, not entering the house. "Don't let him fool you into thinking he doesn't." Wei're rolled his eyes so perfectly, I could imagine him already as a teenager. "Good luck with this heathen." With a ruffling of his hair and a funny face, his sister left him in our inept care.

The ten-year-old walked in as if he had never left, threw the duffel bag on the floor by the couch, and set his laptop on the kitchen counter. He then tipped the corner of his lips upward and said, "You know I have no chickenpox, right? I had it two years ago. You would know if you ever paid any attention." He pointed an accusatory finger toward his brother. "Mom just wants me to spy on you." He threw his head backward and let out a perfect cackle. "Which of course I would so do for free, but she's paying me good money."

My would-be boyfriend was by him in two strides, grabbing the boy by his shoulders, turning him around, and caging him between his chest and his arms. "You little devil," he said, rubbing his knuckles on his brother's jet-black hair. "You will make a great little mercenary in some future war."

The boy thrashed in Li Qiang's arms and tried to bite him, but his brother wouldn't relent. "Let me go, or I will tell Mom you have orgies in your house."

Li Qiang let him go, an expression of utter shock on his face. "What do you know about orgies? You're only ten." *Going on thirty, it seemed.*

"I read, and I watch TV." The boy challenged his brother with a movement of the chin. Li Qiang didn't take the bait, so he crossed his arms and pouted. "I'm hungry. Is there anything good to eat in this house?"

After feeding a seemingly bottomless Wei're, like his brother called him, we sat together on the big couch to watch TV. Li Qiang made sure to sit right next to me, our thighs so close together I could feel his heat. The young man seemed to have already lost any interest in us, with his earbuds stuck in his ears, sitting at the kitchen bar with his laptop. "He'll be in gaming world for the next hour," Li Qiang said with an indulgent smile. "What do you want to watch?"

I'd be perfectly happy just watching him. His thick, dark eyebrows crowning perfectly shaped onyx eyes, the short raven black silk of his hair in stark contrast with his ivory skin… oh boy! I was in so much trouble. Somewhere in the last few days, he had gone from the hot guy in the office who I loved watching from afar to the man who made my heart flutter with just one glance. How was I going to survive until our appearance on the TV show without getting my heart broken into tiny shards?

♥ ♥ ♥

It was beyond awkward. In fact, there wasn't an appropriate adjective to describe the situation after we left Li Wei cuddling under the blankets on the couch and retired to *our* room together. I had roomed with guys before. In college and even afterward, I had been known to share my room with guys during trips to save money. The difference was I hadn't felt a thing but a mild sexual interest for those other guys; while with Li Qiang, the interest gauge was through the roof. Even my toes tingled when he looked at me with those narrow dark eyes.

"This doesn't have to be hard," my fake boyfriend said, an amused grin on his face.

He had dug up the linens and sleeping bag he had stuffed under the bed and was setting a makeshift sleeping area between his real bed and the closet. There wasn't a lot of space on either side of the bed, just enough for him to sleep bookended by the furniture. On the other side there was a bit more room, but I would have to step over him on my way to the bathroom. Gallant as always, Li Qiang dismissed that as a viable spot.

I crossed my arms in defense mode, feeling very

foolish. "I'll just go change, I guess." I grabbed my pajamas—a pair of thin leggings and a long T-shirt—and escaped to the sanctuary of the bathroom. Once there, I closed the door and leaned on it with a big sigh. Shit! What was I doing? This was not the behavior of a grown woman. Long gone were my teen days, and yet here I was acting like one. It took me way too long to get ready for bed, but eventually I emerged in my nightclothes. If you didn't know I was about to go to bed, you would never guess I was in pajamas, yet it felt as if I had just walked in the room wearing a revealing negligee and nothing else.

"Ready," I announced unnecessarily.

Li Qiang had changed into a pair of light blue and white sweats with black spots and a plain white T-shirt. As I got closer, the dark spots on his pants revealed themselves to be penguins. I let out a burst of laughter.

"Are you mocking me?" he asked, pretending to be upset. "What? You don't approve of my save-the-planet pants?"

Shit! Now I liked him even more. He was wearing pants purchased from a charity company. Could he be any more perfect? "No, I love them," I rushed to say. "I was just surprised." He always dressed so conventionally; those penguin pants were a nice surprise.

He turned his mock frown into a smile and dropped to his makeshift bed. "Good, I'm glad you approve of my fashion choices." He threw me a mischievous glance and added, "I don't always wear pj's but when I do, they must mean something."

His attempt at sounding like the Dos Equis guy tickled my funny bone big-time. Tears sprouted from my eyes, and my perfect non-boyfriend laid an index finger over his lips. "Shhh…."

I covered my mouth with the edge of the bed sheet to muffle my chuckles. Too late.

"What's going on in there?" Li Wei was right behind the door, rapping his fingers on the door. "What are you doing?"

Li Qiang shook his head and said, "Nothing, just a joke. Go to bed. It's late."

"No way, I want to come in." To emphasize his words, the young man knocked harder. "Let me in."

Try as I might, I couldn't stop laughing. Li Qiang yelled out, "Or what? You'll blow the door down?" That triggered more giggles. He wriggled his eyebrows with a wicked smile.

There was a moment of silence before his brother answered, "No, but I will make so much noise the neighbors will call the cops."

Laughter suddenly stunted, we looked at each other in alarm. I mouthed the words, "What do we do?"

Li Qiang hopped to his feet and in seconds he had thrown all his bed linens inside the closet and climbed on the bed with me. There was no time to be shocked or to protest; we both slid underneath the sheets and blanket, cozied up together like a true couple and exchanged a here-goes-nothing look.

"Come on in, Wei'er," my lovely intern said. The door had been unlocked all the time. As if guessing my thoughts, he whispered, "There's no lock on the door." My respect for the Li parents went up several notches; that kid was so well trained he didn't burst through doors without being given the permission. Color me impressed!

The boy opened the door and stepped in. He had a grin on his face and a glow in his eyes. "What did I miss?"

The remaining chuckle I had repressed escaped, and I hurried to stifle it with my hands. Li Qiang glowered, a mixture of amusement and disapproval in his eyes. "Nothing, Wei're, she was just making fun of my pajama pants. Why do you have to be so nosy?"

Without any warning, the boy ran and jumped on top of the bed, facing us. "I'm going to tell Mom you guys sleep together." That was exactly what Li Qiang was hoping he would do. Why he wanted to keep his mother under the same illusion as the TV network was beyond me, but he was doing me a huge favor, so I had to go along. "Without being married yet," he added with a wink. Brat! He thought he had something on us.

"We're grown-ups, bro. Mom couldn't care less." I almost laughed, knowing that he was counting on his brother's lack of filter. "Now, go to bed. You're raining on our parade."

He did slide off the bed, but he punctuated it with

kissing noises and a taunt, "Go back to your sloppy kissing, Qiang'er." He left the room, closing the door behind him.

It hit me like an icy fire storm; we were alone and in bed together. My thigh burned and tingled against his. His arm was draped over my shoulders, and his fingers were burning holes in my upper arm. I didn't dare move a finger, and he seemed to be suffering from the same type of paralysis. We sat there like idiots for a good while, neither of us brave enough to say anything or even look at each other. Heat and ice ran wanton through my body, and I was helpless against it.

Li Qiang broke the spell first. "I better make my bed again." He removed his hand from my arm and shoulders, leaving me feeling naked and vulnerable. I fought the urge to reach out and grab his arm or yell out, "Don't go." But he was already off the bed, rubbing his hands over his upper thighs and not meeting my eyes. "Damned brat," he mumbled under his breath as he dug out all the linen from the closet and began spreading it out on the floor. "I apologize for his behavior, Ivy. *Duìbùqǐ*, I'm sorry."

There was no need for him to apologize. I was the one who was sorry; sorry I was older than he was, sorry he was now lying on the floor instead of the bed, sorry our relationship was fictional. I guess my father was right all along; I was just a total screwup.

♡ ♡ ♡

An hour and ten years later, I was still awake, my eyes fixed on the ceiling fan, a modern white contraption that blended with the background. It wasn't on, so it was much like watching grass grow, but it was either that or turn on my side to watch beautiful Li Qiang sleep. My heart hadn't slowed down since the moment he slid off the bed to stretch on his linen nest. I didn't dare to check, but by the sound of his slow breathing, I could tell he was asleep.

I sighed. *This is stupid.* I could turn the other way. Chiding myself for not having thought of it, I turned to the side, fluffing the pillow under my head. I had to make sure I woke up before he did in the morning. I couldn't risk him seeing me with messy hair and spittle dripping from my mouth. What if I snored? Worse, what if I farted while I slept? Oh my God, I would never fall asleep this way. I tossed to the other side, forgetting my fake boyfriend was there and then tried to toss back, but throwing the pillow off the bed instead.

The flying pillow hit Li Qiang right on the face. Shit! What was wrong with me? He mumbled something and then sat up, eyes shrunk by sleep. "What happened?" I considered pretending to be asleep, but I couldn't even move. He stared at me, pillow in his hand and yawned. "Why are you attacking me with this weapon of mass softness?"

Despite my mortification, a smile twitched on my lips. "Sorry. I was turning, and I guess I did it a bit too enthusiastically." It sounded like a question, so I shrugged. I had gone soft in the head. "Did I hurt you?"

He shook his head and rose on his knees. "My feelings maybe." He laughed and semi-crawled toward the bed. "Shall I teach you how to use a pillow?" That mischievous smile of his was back.

In a fluid move, he was on his feet, pillow still in his hands. He sat on the edge of the bed and bent over me to place the pillow under my head. Our faces came so close I could feel the warmth of his breath. My heart stopped. I'm not kidding; it actually stopped for a fraction of a second. If I moved even an inch, I could kiss him. I wanted to, I so wanted to. He spared me of the need to decide by brushing his warm lips over mine. It was barely a kiss, but it left me breathless and stunned. Liquid fire was running amok inside my veins, spreading to each cell of my body. I was about to self-combust.

Hovering over my hungry lips, Li Qiang whispered, "Sorry, I shouldn't have." Since my brain—in ferocious battle with my heart—couldn't decide whether I was also sorry or not, I made a weird guttural sound and nodded. "I shouldn't have."

I had dived so deeply into his eyes I couldn't see anything or understand why he kept repeating that. "No, you shouldn't," I finally squeaked out and immediately wished I hadn't. Maybe it was wrong, our lips touching and bodies so close it was impossible to disguise our desire for each other, but it felt right. He didn't move. "Why aren't you moving?" I didn't want him to, but he really should. I wondered for a moment if this was how it felt to have multiple personalities, arguing with yourself, having totally contradictory wishes and feelings.

He smiled then, but his voice was husky, thick with want. "I can't. You're holding me."

When had that happened? Why were my arms holding him tightly on the spot? Mortified, I loosened my hold on him and dropped my hands to my sides. "Sorry," I said, breathlessly. "I didn't realize I was doing that."

Li Qiang, now freed from my vise-like grasp, straightened and looked at me from between half-closed eyelids. "Nothing to apologize for. I enjoyed every second of it." Cheeky monkey. Was he mocking me? He did have a cat-who-ate-the-canary expression on his handsome face. "Maybe we should do that more often."

What in heaven's name did he mean by that? I sat up in bed, ready to ask him, but he had already dropped to his sleeping nook and turned away from me.

"Sleep tight," he murmured, his voice muffled by the blanket he had pulled up to his nose.

Yeah, right! Like I was going to be able to sleep at all after that.

CHAPTER TEN

BUSTED

I made my escape while Li Qiang was busy fighting with his brother over scrambled eggs. My pretense at being asleep had worked like a charm, and he left me alone in the room long enough to get dressed, grab my purse, and leave with a wave and a squeaky, "See you at work." I didn't give him time to point out it was super early; my plan was to swing by my place and take a shower before going to the office. After last night's accidental-on-purpose kiss, I was not looking forward to facing the man who had stolen my heart. Yes, I had finally admitted to myself that I was head over heels in love with my wonderful young intern and that no amount of denial or self-blaming was going to change that fact.

By the time I made it to the office, I was calmer—due in part to two shots of espresso and a should-beillegal dark chocolate Frappuccino. Amber Lee was already buried in her work and barely noticed my arrival until I placed an aromatic cup of coffee in front of her nose. She gave it a long sniff with her eyes closed and then drank about half of the contents in one big gulp. I cringed. The coffee was hot, but I knew my friend was extremely tolerant to heat.

"Good?" I asked, my head tilted to watch her as she took in the flavor of the roasted magic beans.

She fluttered her eyelashes without opening her eyes. "Divine." She sighed and took another whiff, holding the cup in both hands reverently. "This is why I love you, Ivory Bee."

Satisfied that she was awake and not burned, I sat down on a chair close by and peeled off my pink, knee-length duster. "So what you're saying is that if I didn't bring you coffee in the morning you would not be my friend." I had taken a long, hot shower and changed into more professional clothes than the raggedy jeans and T-shirt I had slipped into at Li Qiang's house. "I see how you are."

Amber Lee opened her eyes and smiled at me. "You know I'd love you even without coffee," she purred, sneaking in another sniff of the brew. "But it's a perk."

I had to laugh. "I need you to distract me with a ton of work today," I told her, pulling the long sleeves of my boho blouse up to my elbows. "Maybe even send me on a field mission."

She blinked and tilted her head. "You want

me to send you on a hunt? For animals or eligible bachelors?" She had lowered her voice to make it sound skeptical. "I'm not catching your drift, boss." I let out an exaggerated sigh. "Ah, trouble in honeymoon paradise?"

"Don't call it that," I warned her, picking on invisible threads on my black pants. "We might have had an awkward moment last night."

She perked up at that, scooting all the way to the edge of her chair and leaning forward, the coffee cup still in her hands. "Awkward? As in no-pants awkward? Do tell." She was evil.

"No, we may have…." Her eyes widened and her lips puckered. I might as well come clean. "We briefly kissed."

My friend straightened like a rod. "Like, each other?"

I threw my head back and sighed again. "No, like the walls." I lifted my head again and glared. "Of course each other." Before she could get too excited, I added, "It was a tiny kiss—really barely qualified as one. But now I don't even want to look at him. I'm too embarrassed."

"Who exactly initiated that not-quite-a-kiss?" Forever nosy.

"He did, but I wanted him to." Okay, my teenage self was back controlling this thirty-six-year-old body. "I can't face him."

She raised a hand, palm facing me. "Wait! He

kissed you, and you are embarrassed? Why? Because you liked it?" I nodded, and she shook her head. "You gotta be kidding me. How old are you anyway? Twelve?" I must have looked so miserable, she leaned over again and patted my hand. "All right, I will take care of it. God forbid you have to face the guy you have the hots for."

As if on cue, Li Qiang walked in, his backpack over his light jacket. As soon as our eyes met, the smile I so loved dawned on his lips. "Morning, boss." He waved as if we hadn't just seen each other a couple of hours ago. "Hi, Amber Lee." He was the only one in the office who dared call my friend by her first name. Maybe because she would always smile at him instead of the scowl she offered everybody else.

"Hi, handsome," my friend said in a singing tone while wiggling her fingers in the air. "Slept well?" I kicked her shins and opened my eyes as wide as I could. She didn't even flinch. "I hear there was some excitement at your house last night." Oh, I was so going to kill her!

To his credit, Li Qiang didn't take the bait. He dropped his backpack to the floor by his desk and opened his laptop. "Yes, unexpected visitor." Amber Lee threw me a cartoonish eyebrow raise. I shrugged. I hadn't had the chance to tell her about Li Wei yet. "My brother and his imaginary chickenpox."

"Wait, brother? Chickenpox? Visitor?" It was as if she had the hiccups. I would have laughed if I wasn't so anxious to change the subject. Quickly.

I opened my mouth to explain, but my intern beat me to it. "My mom sent my brother to make sure we were really a couple." *Oh boy, here it comes.* "Ivy and I had to sleep in the same room." Shit. At least he didn't say that we had slept together. I lowered my eyes and became fascinated by the tip of my boots.

"In the same room?" I knew she wouldn't let it slide. This was Amber Lee we were talking about, Master Plotter extraordinaire, especially when it came to setting me up with a guy. Admittedly, she was looking out for my happiness, considering she thought I needed some romance in my life. "How come you've neglected to tell me that detail, boss?" Even though I was still staring at that little water stain on my boot, I could feel her eyes burning on me. "Did anything… *interesting* happen while you were sharing your sleeping quarters?" *Damn you, Amber Lee!*

"Boss threw a pillow at me during the night," Li Qiang said with a chuckle. "Not sure she was trying to wake me up or just releasing some anger." *Bless his beautiful heart.* Shit, now I loved him even more.

Amber Lee gave me an approving nod. "You guys are boring." With that final assessment, my friend turned her chair around and went back to work.

I stood up, retrieved my duster from the back of the chair, and headed to my office. Before I could open the door though, Li Qiang's hand covered mine on the knob. Startled, I looked up at him and met his smiling eyes. "What?" I asked, my hand burning pleasantly under his.

He leaned in and whispered, "Thank you." I blinked. "For the kiss."

Before I could react, he moved away and left me there, half paralyzed, mouth agape. Why was he thanking me? I'm the one who should thank him; that brief, barely there kiss had been the most exciting one ever. The problem now was I wanted more. So much more.

♥ ♥ ♥

At some point, I had to return home—or, in this case, to Li Qiang's home. I did my best to procrastinate; I browsed the local bookstore, had a cup or two of coffee at Starbucks, bought treats at the grocery store, ate ice cream at the corner shop, and even walked around the mall for a while—something I totally abhorred. But it was already getting dark, and knowing my roommate, he was probably waiting for me with dinner he had ordered on the way home from work. He was sweet and thoughtful like that. So I got in the car and drove to his place.

Laden with bags of shopping I didn't need, I entered the elevator to his floor and balanced the bags in my arms, trying to ring the doorbell. I had expected Li Qiang, but Wei'er opened the door instead, his face bright with excitement and a touch of mischief. "Guess who's here?" he blurted out before I could say anything. I tried to peek behind him, but this ten-year-old was almost as tall as me already. "The TV people."

I nearly dropped all the bags on my toes. The TV network was here? Now? I knew they would be coming soon but—shit, shit, shit!

Teresa Lord's artificial smile appeared next to our fake-chickenpox patient. "Well, hello, stranger," she said, her polished, honeyed voice sticking to my ears like molasses. "You took your time to get home, didn't you?"

I tried to talk, I really did, but all I could utter were weird, incoherent sounds. Li Qiang came to my rescue, slipping past the TV anchorwoman and relieving me of the bags. "Ms. Lord granted us the honor of her visit," he explained, his eyes saying what his words did not, "The bitch showed up unannounced." He carried the bags into the living room, and I followed him blindly, still speechless. "I called you several times, but you didn't answer."

Crap. I had turned off the phone as yet another avoidance method. "I was at the mall," I finally squeaked out. "They have terrible signal reception there."

Li Qiang placed the bags on the floor by the couch, and in a one-step stride, he was next to me, his arm sliding over my lower back and hooking onto my hip. I whipped my head around to look at him, but he silenced me with a kiss—a brief touch of the lips that made all the tension in my body melt away like a caramel in the oven. I may have hung on to him longer than I had to, afraid my jellied legs wouldn't hold me.

"Oh so sweet," Teresa crooned. She turned to her camera man and added, "Lloyd, did you get that?" Holy crap, they had the camera rolling the whole time. "Your fiancé was telling me how his brother is staying with you for a while."

A lifeline! "Yes, and he has the chickenpox so you better come back another time." I sounded like a frantic parrot.

Teresa laughed, the mirth never quite reaching her eyes. "I had it as a kid, and so did Lloyd, so we're fine." Damn it. I guess they were here to stay. "Don't let us stop you from your usual routine. That's what the public wants to see."

My boyfriend dropped his arm and said, "I have dinner ready, *gūniáng*." He had set up the table and a succulent scent teased my nostrils. "Will you join us for dinner, Ms. Lord?"

The TV woman shook her head, her hair not budging at all. "God no. I'm on a very special diet." She looked at me as if looking at a piece of rotten meat. "You go ahead and eat your normal stuff."

The three of us sat at Li Qiang's small rectangular table, my not-quite boyfriend being careful enough to sit next to me and across from his brother who was still gawking at Teresa, his mouth wide open. I couldn't resist; I stretched across the table, placed two fingers under his chin, and closed it. He looked at me half confused, half surprised, so I winked at him. "Didn't want you to swallow a bug," I told him. His cheeks turned crimson, but he was gracious enough to smile at me.

Li Qiang had brought home a variety of Chinese dishes I didn't recognize. He seemed to read the question in my eyes and said, "My mom insisted on cooking for us today." He leaned over and whispered in my ear, "I hope you like Chinese. The real stuff, not the delivery crap."

The touch of his lips against my skin caused a surge of heat to my neck, and I tried to disguise it by grabbing a pair of the chopsticks on the table and digging in. Everything looked delicious, and I couldn't decide what to eat first. In a gesture that mirrored what I had seen his dad do for his mom, Li Qiang picked a steamed bun from one of the platters in the middle of the table and placed it on my plate, followed by a couple of shrimp and steamed baby bok choy. Another layer of my heart melted. I mimicked him and placed a few items on his plate and smiled at him, hoping he got my silent message, "Thank you."

It was weird to eat while being filmed. I hoped to God I didn't have anything stuck to my teeth, because I couldn't stop smiling at my wonderful boyfriend. Wait! When had I started thinking of him as my boyfriend? Not fake boyfriend, just *boyfriend*. I was going to need therapy after that.

After dinner, Wei'er seemed to have finally snapped

out of his fangirling stasis and settled on the armchair by the window, his legs draped over one of the arms, ready to play with his Switch. My boyfriend—*oh shit, here I go again*—and I went to the kitchen to clean up. While he wrapped the leftovers and stored them in the fridge, I began rinsing the dirty dishes. I almost jumped out of my skin when I felt a body against mine; Li Qiang's side brushed my hip. I looked up and locked eyes with him. He smiled and stuck out a hand as if asking for something. For a moment I was lost; what the hell was he trying to say? Then it dawned on me; I handed him the rinsed dinnerware one at a time, and he placed them in the dishwasher. That simple, everyday activity made me glow inside; it was intimate and sweet. And I didn't want it to be over. For the first time in my life, I was actually enjoying doing dishes.

He held out a towel to me, and I dried up my hands, never once dropping my eyes from his. A strong, magnetic field had been growing between and around us, and now that the chore was finished, Li Qiang had gotten closer and closer to me until our bodies touched. I looked up at his eyes, so dark and warm, and lost it. I literally lost my marbles; I cupped the back of his neck with a hand, pulled his face closer to mine, and kissed him. Full-frontal, lip-to-lip action. Every inch of my body tingled and softened as I hung boneless from his arms.

"Perfect!" Our lips drew apart abruptly. How had I forgotten the camera crew was still there? Oh God, they had been recording that kiss. "That was panty-melting indeed."

Li Qiang's still dazed eyes widened at her words. "Shh, there's a ten-year-old in the room." The ten-year-old in question was so focused on his game, the world could have collapsed around him and he would have never noticed.

My heart was beating in my ears, and I couldn't catch my breath. What had I done? What in heaven's name had come over me? What would Li Qiang think of me? "Sorry, I didn't mean—" My boyfriend smiled at me then, and all the mortification of a moment ago morphed into desire. I wanted him. "Coffee?" I asked stupidly.

The crew didn't stay for long, and as soon as Teresa was out the door, after promising to contact us within the next few days with more news about the show, Li Qiang reached for my hand. Neither of us spoke, our eyes doing all the talking while we sat and stared at whatever was playing on TV, waiting for his brother to go to bed. I excused myself as Li Qiang was setting his brother up for the night, thinking I'd get in my pajamas and brush my teeth. Turns out I couldn't; my mind was too full of Xiǎoli, full of his scent and his taste and how he felt against me. I sat on the edge of the bed, staring at the door like a fool and incapable of doing anything else.

When the door opened a bit later—no idea how much later—and my handsome, tall, and slim boyfriend came through, my heart exploded into a tap dance that robbed me of air. He closed the door behind him and stood there, his back against the cold wood, questioning me with his eyes. I gave him a tentative smile, my lips trembling as they kicked up in the corners, and he smiled back with a sigh. I raised my hand in his direction, inviting him closer.

"Wei're is asleep," he said in a whisper. He took a breath and asked, "Are you sure?"

Before I could change my mind, I hopped out of bed and threw myself into his arms. "Never been so sure in my whole life."

♡ ♡ ♡

I had always enjoyed silence. Even as a child, I had quickly concluded that silence was like ice cream, with many different flavors and varying degrees of quality. There was the cheap off-brand vanilla that tasted like old powdered milk and the butter pecan that tasted of sunshine and laughter. The silence that fell between Xiǎoli and me was a rich dark chocolate covered in sweet whipped cream and drizzled with melted milk chocolate. I hung from his neck, toes barely touching the floor, eyes glued to his obsidian pupils. Bliss. Pure, unadulterated bliss.

My boyfriend first broke the silence. "You're beautiful, you know?" I shook my head, but my heart danced to the tune of his words. "I've been crushing on you since the moment you told me to walk into your office a few months ago."

"You never said anything." My vocal cords were constricted by the thrill of it all—the heat of his hard body squashed against mine, his scent, his eyes....

"You're my boss," he said with a soft chuckle, his smile warming every inch of me. "It was slightly intimidating."

I laughed. "I'm flattered that you find me intimidating." He leaned his head forward and planted a kiss on my nose. "My father always says I am wimpier than Mr. Wimpy."

"Who?" His eyebrows arched above his eyes.

"Popeye's friend?" He raised his brows even higher. "You got to be kidding. You don't know who Popeye is?"

"The food chain?" I couldn't tell if he was serious or giving me a hard time. He was young, after all; I was old enough to remember the old cartoon my mother often watched with me and used as an excuse to convince me to eat my spinach.

"You really don't know?" Would this kind of thing be a common occurrence with the two of us? Something that clearly showed our difference in age. My heart sank, and I slumped in his arms.

Li Qiang burst out laughing. "You're too gullible, *gūniáng*. I know exactly who Popeye's friend is." He kissed my nose again. "But you are not a wimp." His warm lips traveled to my cheek. "You are strong." My earlobe. "Brave." His lips returned to my cheek, fluttering over the jaw to the corner of my mouth. "Smart." He hovered over my lips, teasingly. "And you have the most beautiful brown eyes."

Parts of me had liquefied already, and if he didn't hurry up, I might just end up in a puddle at his feet. "Will you kiss me already?"

He pulled away for a second, amusement in his glance. "So bossy." He smiled in earnest then. "I like it."

I didn't wait any longer and crossed the short space between our lips. Unavoidable mortification would come later, I was sure, but for now I wanted to let go, to free this yearning, this fire Li Qiang had lit inside me. If it burned me to a crisp, so be it.

My frantic kiss slowed down and mellowed as his tongue met mine. Definitely dark chocolate and strong coffee. I explored deeper, only too happy to either swallow him or be swallowed. My fingers were buried in his thick, silky hair, and his hands had ventured under the lower hem of my T-shirt, boldly traveling up my sides to areas where no man had gone in a while. I thought I moaned inside his mouth, but it could have been him. We were so entangled in each other it was hard to tell.

The flame, that pilot light that I had been carrying around for a while now had turned into a full-blast tundra fire. I pulled away from him just long enough to grab hold of his shirt to untuck it from his pants. My lips were having a hard time staying apart from his for long, so the stripping that followed was clumsy and awkward. I struggled with the buttons, feeling very tempted to do what you often saw in romance movies and just tear the buttons off. I could buy him a new shirt afterward, couldn't I? In the end, he saved me from the decision, and with deft fingers, he removed the shirt himself. I took a step backward, my hand flat on his bare chest, to watch him. My boyfriend had a nice six-pack, strong, lean chest muscles, and a tantalizing, hot-as-hell Adonis belt—you know, that vee in the hip area that Amber Lee always called the arrow because it pointed at… never mind. The sight fanned the raging fire in my lower regions, and I had the urgent need to be naked, skin to skin with that beautiful man.

Li Qiang hesitated for a moment before pulling my T-shirt over my head and throwing it up in the air. I reached behind my back and unhooked my bra, my eyes never leaving his in a challenge; my ex had always said my breasts were too small to be sexy. Now I stood bare in front of a much younger man I was falling in love with, and that fear, that tiny critical voice that permanently lived inside of me had quieted down, waiting for his reaction.

Li Qiang lowered is gaze from my defiant eyes to my chest, lingered there for a moment before coming up again. "Can I touch you?" His plea was uttered in a strangled voice. I nodded, and he took another step toward me, his hand cupping my breast. I moaned, the roughness of his palms sending shivers down my spine. "It fits perfectly in my hand," he sighed out as he reverently covered the sensitive skin with his hand. "You're so beautiful, *gūniáng*."

I moaned again, whether in relief he found me pleasing or pleasure from his touch, I couldn't be sure. Probably both. I held his free hand to my other breast and almost swooned, parts of me throbbing in anticipation. So far from being rational or cautious, I unzipped his pants and tried to pull them down. Not sure what happened next, but a few moments later we were both naked, the back of my legs against the edge of the bed and Li Qiang's mouth latched to mine. Gently, he pushed me down flat on the bed and slid over me, his taut skin rubbing against mine. I know I heard crackling, and I certainly felt the heat.

His hands and his eyes found my breasts again. The hunger in his gaze was exhilarating. Let's face it; I had lusted over him for a long while, but I never once thought he returned the feeling. Now, the spark in his piercing eyes told me otherwise. He wanted me as badly as I wanted him.

When his mouth followed his hands and suckled my breast, I couldn't handle it anymore. With a swift move, I flipped us and straddled him, swooning at the swelling heat I felt underneath me. *Oh yes! He wants me.*

"Hell, *gūniáng*," he said, his voice coming in breathless gasps. "When did this happen?"

"What do you mean? You're sexy and sweet,"

I replied, just as breathless. "What girl in that office hasn't dreamed of being where I am right now?" My mouth was very busy smothering him with kisses along his strong chin and his neck, and my voice came out muffled. Just as well since all I was saying was crap.

Li Qiang pushed me away from him for a moment, staring at me in surprise. "All the girls? Are you serious?"

I laughed. "Stop being so modest. You know that's true," I said. He could not have possibly missed the batting of lashes and the soft sighs every time he entered the office. "Can we stop talking and get back to business?"

With an inhaled chuckle, he swallowed my mouth in a frenzied kiss as if trying to make up for lost time and rolled me under him again.

"God, I love the way you taste." He was not kidding. His mouth trailed kisses down my chest and kept on going down in a toe-curling mission to show me just how much he loved my flavor. When his lips found their target between my legs, I arched against his mouth, slightly delirious with pleasure, wondering what I had done to deserve such tender ministrations. That's when I heard it.

I thought I had imagined it at first, but the second time the knocking was louder and more assertive. "What are you guys doing in there? Why are you fighting?" Holy shit! For all the angels in heaven, Wei're was right behind the door, trying to get in.

Behind the *unlocked* door.

I just about died. What if he decided we were in danger or something and forgot his family's rules of never opening a door without being asked to enter? Forgetting that his brother was between my legs, fiercely working on making me feel well-loved and wanted, I kicked my legs and scooted up the soft surface, slamming my knee on the side of his head. No way I was stopping to check on what damage I had done. Not while a small human was separated from this erotic scene by only a thin door and his good manners.

Like a coiled wire, I bounced off the bed and stood, searching for clothes, any clothes, to cover my naked body. I skittered around like Scrat, the squirrel from *Ice Age*, looking for the elusive nut in vain. I stood naked and terrified, hyperventilating and now also mortified I had somehow attacked the one man I had drooled over for the past few weeks.

Li Qiang was on all fours on the bed, his hand flattened on his face and moaning. "Oh my God, Xiǎoli," I exclaimed, snapping out of my terrified stupor and kneeling beside him. "Are you okay?"

When he raised his face to look at me, I almost fell on my bare butt. I had given him a black eye. Well, it wasn't black yet, but it would be. Around his gorgeous left eye there was an alarmingly red welt that seemed to be growing as I watched it. "Crap! I'm so sorry."

He burst out laughing. "You really are trying to kill me, aren't you, Ivy?" he said between chuckles. "If you didn't want me to taste you, all you had to do was say something. You didn't have to kick me in the eye."

I didn't know what to do. Should I put some clothes on and run out to get ice or just get a wet towel from the bathroom? What about the munchkin outside the door who kept banging his fists and screaming Li Qiang's name in a panic? Were we really that noisy to make him think we were fighting?

"We're not fighting, Wei're," my battered boyfriend yelled out at the door before turning his eyes back to mine. "Put your pajamas on. He'll never give up until he can make sure we haven't killed each other."

While I rushed to dig up some pajamas out of the dresser—I couldn't find the ones I had been wearing—Li Qiang slipped out of the bed and went to the bathroom. Once I was presentable, I opened the door to a terrified young man; Li Wei's face was wet with tears and his eyes swollen. He fell into my arms, sobbing.

"Honey, we're fine. We weren't fighting at all, just playing around." No matter how many times I repeated that mantra, the boy just wouldn't calm down. "Your brother is in the bathroom. He'll be out in a minute."

Baffled was an understatement for what I was feeling in that moment. Even if we were a bit loud with our expressions of pleasure, why would the boy be so afraid we'd be fighting?

Li Qiang finally emerged from the bathroom, and I couldn't help it, I gasped. It was going to be hard to convince Wei're we weren't fighting with his brother's eye already swollen almost shut.

♥ ♥ ♥

If anyone had told me a month or so ago that I'd be lying in bed with a much younger man and his brother asleep between us I would have told them they were nuts. Yet, there I was doing exactly that. Wei're had finally fallen asleep, stretched out in our bed, his small face stained with tears, one of his hands still clutched tightly to mine.

Li Qiang, left eye turning a scary shade of purple and wearing his penguin pajamas—how had he found them amid the confusion?—watched me as I gently pulled my hand from his brother's grip. "I thought he was getting better," he said, planting a brief kiss on Li Wei's forehead. "He must have had a dream or something. We weren't making that much noise." He lifted his eyes to mine. "Were we?"

Heat rose to my cheeks. *Oh God! Let's not talk about it.* I shook my head. "No, I don't think so." In my mind, I revisited the scene, looking for maybe an accidental bump into the dresser or dropping a knickknack on the floor. It just didn't happen. Then again, all I could remember were Li Qiang's lips and tongue on me. I diverted. "What caused the panic attack?"

With a sigh, Li Qiang draped a blanket over his brother. "Wei're suffers from PTSD." I tilted my head to the side. "It's a long story."

Oh no, he wasn't going to get away that easy. "I would love to hear it." I thought he flinched a little. That was a first. Li Qiang was not as immune to stress as he looked, after all. "Please."

He threw a glance at his brother before settling against the pillow. "A couple years ago, I took him on a road trip to Disney. We had a great time, but on the way back we got caught in a storm. It came at us out of nowhere." He raked his fingers through his hair and licked his lips. My eyes followed his other hand as he unconsciously sought out his little brother's. "There was debris flying all around us, hitting the car left and right. Wei're was terrified." He paused, his eyes lost in space. "Fuck, *I* was terrified. When the post of a wooden fence broke through the windshield it nearly impaled my brother." A shiver shook the lovely man beside me. "I took my eyes from the road and lost control of the car. We rolled so many times, I lost count. I was only aware of my head hitting against the window over and over again and the hysterical screams of my brother."

I reached out for him, covering his and Li Wei's hand with mine. Guilt filled me; why had I brought up such a difficult memory? Despite his obvious pain, Li Qiang continued, "The next thing I knew, I was coming to, still attached to my seat by the seat belt but upside down, warm blood dripping over my eyes. Wei're was awake, shaking uncontrollably." His quiet voice shook. Pausing for a moment, he took a deep breath. "The poor kid had a broken leg—a really bad break—

but had never lost consciousness. You can imagine his terror. He couldn't even talk, just sat there with his head where his butt should have been, bloodied and soaking wet from the rain that still battered the car."

"Oh my God, that must have been so traumatic for both of you," I whispered, rubbing my thumb on the top of his hand. "How long did it take for someone to find you?"

He shook his head slowly and shrugged. "I honestly don't know. It could have been a few minutes or hours." His eyes roamed over to his brother again, who was thankfully fast asleep, his breath back to the slow rhythm of slumber. "It felt like years. Eventually I was able to grab my seat belt emergency cutter that miraculously was still stuck inside the door compartment, cut myself free, and stand upright. The storm was finally past, even though rain still fell heavily at times, so I brought my brother out of the car to lay him down on the grass." He stopped again, swallowed hard, his Adam's apple bobbing on his neck. "I couldn't believe it. It was a miracle we were alive; the storm or whatever it was, threw the car at least a quarter of a mile off the road and into a ravine. A few more feet and we would have drowned in the raging river."

His voice caught, and I jumped out of bed to come around to his side. I slipped behind him and spooned him, my arms going around his waist and my hands flat on his chest. His heart was pumping so hard, I swore it felt as if it was trying to explode out of his chest. I pulled myself as close to him as I could, my face on the back of his shoulder. "You don't have to tell me the rest if you don't want to, Xiǎoli," I whispered against his T-shirt.

"It's okay. I want you to know," he said, a hand covering and fingers interlacing with mine. "Paramedics came at some point. Because of the storm, they were looking for victims. By then I wasn't completely aware of what was happening. I had lost a lot of blood and was hypothermic. I woke up in the hospital a day or so later."

With another squeeze, I pressed my lips against the fabric that covered his back and kissed him. "What kind of injuries did you guys have?"

His chest filled and emptied a couple times before he answered. "I had a cracked skull, concussion, lots of scrapes and bruises but nothing incurable or long lasting. Wei're had a horrible break on his fibula, right below his knee, a broken wrist and some other smaller injuries. It took a few surgeries and a lot of PT for him to be able to walk normal again."

"So he freaks out when he hears certain noises?" I asked, still not clear about what had triggered his reaction.

He took a peek over his shoulder and smiled, a poor imitation of his usual ones. "He must have had a dream. He's been a little anxious about school, and when his anxieties get the best of him, he starts having nightmares and wakes up in a panic thinking it's true."

I was still confused. "He kept saying we were fighting."

"After the accident, my family had a lot of fights," he explained in a hushed voice. "I felt guilty because I was driving, my mom felt guilty because she had rushed us home to celebrate my sister's birthday, my sister felt guilty that it was her birthday that made us drive that day." He sighed. "We were all stressed and angry—not really at each other but at the situation—and we were fighting all the time. Families do that sometimes. That's when I moved out."

"And Wei're thought you were leaving because of him."

"We needed some space," he said with a sad chuckle. "It worked though; things calmed down and went back to normal. But Wei're was never the same."

"Neither were you," I said, comprehension dawning on me. "That's why you don't drive."

Li Qiang turned around slowly, careful not to wake up his brother, and looked me in the eye. "Now you know the skeleton in my closet. What's yours?"

I studied his beautifully shaped eyes, the smooth bridge of his nose, the fullness and contour of his lips and decided it was time he knew. "My skeleton?" I swallowed hard, my mouth dry. "I'm never good enough."

CHAPTER ELEVEN

EGGS AND BURNED BACON

I could do this. I released the pressure in my shoulders, shook my arms a few times, and then glanced at what was before me. I counted a dozen eggs, a whole package of bacon, one green pepper, an onion, a tomato, shredded cheese, and some spices. I could do this; I would conquer breakfast. With one wipe of the hands on my leggings, I grabbed the knife and attacked the pepper, the onion, and the tomato with the ferocity and determination of a Marine on a mission. Once the three vegetables were nicely chopped, I turned my attention to the bacon. The slime of the fat always made me gag, but I held my breath, opened the package and lined up each slice on a foil-lined oven dish. I slid the pan in the oven, closed the door and started one of the burners to heat up a large frying pan.

So far so good. I definitely can do this.

Once the veggies were pan-frying, I broke the eggs into a small bowl and whipped them. *Whipped them good.* The song echoing in my head made me sway my hips and do a little tap dance. We hadn't finished what we'd started last night, but my soul felt the lightest in years. Could that pitter-patter inside my chest be happiness? A sprinkle of parsley, salt, and pepper, and my eggs were ready to be poured over the soft veggies.

Cracking open the oven, I took a peek at the sizzling bacon. *You don't scare me, you porky lard.* I was the master of the kitchen. Deciding it needed a few more minutes, I closed the door and tended to the omelet. It looked perfect, and I only hoped it would taste just as good. I turned off the burner and sprinkled the eggs with lots of cheese before covering the pan with a lid. I was just about to check the bacon again when my phone, lying on the counter, danced across the granite surface.

"Hello?" I said before realizing I hadn't checked the caller ID. It better not be a telemarketer. "Ivory Tower speaking."

"That ridiculous name. Who takes you serious with a name like that?" My father's acidic voice burned in my ears, and my stomach fell. *You gave me this name, Father.*

"Father? What do you need?" He rarely called me unless it was time for our monthly lunches, and that was still almost two weeks away. "Did something happen?"

"I need to talk to you." I could hear traffic in the background, so he was most likely on his way to the office, smack in the middle of the busiest blocks in the city. "There is something we must discuss without delay."

Despite it all, I was curious; what could be so important my father would break with tradition to want to see me before our regular time? "Are you sick, Father?" He looked as if he was in perfect health the last time I'd seen him, but he was over sixty after all.

"I'm perfectly fine," he said as if I had suggested he was a thief. "Meet me Tuesday for lunch." On a weekday? Another break in tradition. What was going on?

"The usual spot?"

"Yes, at noon. Don't be late." I sighed, confused and a bit worried. "Ivory Marie, you never cease to surprise me."

My heart leapt in my chest. Was my father about to praise me? "What do you mean?"

"The stupid and ill-advised things you do, Ivory." My heart fell with a thump, and I couldn't breathe. "You are such a disappointment. When are you going to make me proud?" I had no idea what he was talking about, but I could take my pick. For my father, even my choice of shoes or makeup were misguided disasters. Tears burned in my eyes. "When are you going to be a true Tower instead of a Logan? You have my genes in you. Why do you always use your mother's?"

I didn't say anything. I couldn't. Tears were rolling down my face and collecting around my nostrils and the corner of my lips. If I tried to open my mouth, I'd sob, and I couldn't give him that satisfaction.

"Tuesday at noon. Do not be late." With that command, my father hung up on me.

I stood with the phone still by my ear, trying to control myself. Why did I let my father have that effect on me? I didn't need him anymore. I was an adult, a successful businesswoman with my own independent life. I could afford to let him go, and yet, I couldn't. I wanted him to love me, to be proud of me, to be the father I always envied my friends for.

A warm smell hit my nose, and I wiped the tears with the back of my hand. Through the haze of my emotional turmoil, I sensed something wrong. But what was it?

"Is something burning?" Li Qiang's voice snapped me out of my confusion.

I sniffed the air, looked around and belatedly ran to take the bacon out from the oven—black and smoky, like pieces of wood in a fireplace. My bacon was burned to a crisp. I placed the tray on top of the stove as Li Qiang approached. It was all ruined. I burst out crying, my tears falling directly over the charred meat.

Li Qiang ran the last few steps toward me and held my hands. "Why are you crying? It's just bacon. We'll be okay."

"I wanted to surprise you with breakfast," I

sniveled, snot running freely from my nose. "And I burnt it all. I'm good for nothing."

Warm arms enveloped me and pulled me close. My boyfriend cupped the back of my head and gently pressed it against his chest. "What are you saying, Ivy? You're amazing. Burning bacon doesn't make you a failure, you know?" I cried louder. "What makes you think you are no good? Did I say something to make you feel that way?"

I shook my head. "My father called," I admitted between sobs. "He thinks I'm worthless." Shit, I sounded like a twelve-year-old, leaving snot tracks in my lovely intern's T-shirt. "My father hates me."

Li Qiang was quiet for a heartbeat. "Sweetheart, your father is a cruel man," he whispered in my ear, gravel in his voice. "He should be proud of you and instead chooses to berate you about everything. What did he want?"

Getting a better control over myself, I told him about our conversation on the phone. "I can't imagine what he wants to talk about."

He twisted and bit his upper lip. "Do you think he found out about the TV stunt?" Shit. I hadn't thought about that. I closed my eyes for a moment, regrouping. Was that what he wanted to see me about? Had he heard the rumors of my fake engagement? But he had already met Li Qiang, so that could not have come as a surprise to him. What freaking bee had flown under his bonnet now?

I straightened in his arms and sniffled a bit. "Might as well eat what I managed not to burn," I said with an attempt at a smile. "Unless you like blackened bacon."

Li Qiang's face opened into a smile. "Leave the bacon for Wei're," he said. "That kid will eat just about anything."

As if on cue, Li Wei emerged from the bedroom, his black hair sticking up in all directions. He stopped a few steps into the living room, scratched his head, rubbed his eyes, and then said, "I'm starved. Do you have any bacon?"

My boyfriend and I exchanged a look, glanced at his baby brother, and burst out laughing. I'd worry about my father later.

♥ ♥ ♥

Later came a lot sooner than I thought. Not the later when I would have to think about my next meeting with my father, but the later when I had to face what had happened the night before; Li Qiang and I had been intimate. Holy shit, his tongue and lips had been on my—Hell had nothing on the fire burning my face and neck when we finally all sat down to eat breakfast.

Maybe I'd just avoid the subject altogether. "Wei're, how are you feeling today?"

Li Wei paused, his forkful of eggs hovering over the plate for a second or two. "I'm fine," he said, shoveling the eggs into his mouth. "A little scratchy," he added, bits of food escaping and flying out of his lips. "Must be the chickenpox." The little devil had the nerve to wink at me, knowing all too well it was fake.

I hadn't been referring to that. We all knew Mom Li had made that up, but I had to give him credit for remembering his mother's instructions. He pretended to scratch his armpit and then resumed his eating. I repressed a chuckle and automatically glanced at his brother.

Big mistake!

His eyes were already on me, warm and full of promise. I swallowed, swiped the coffee mug from the table, and took a large gulp of the hot brew to disguise my discomfort.

Li Qiang smiled and reached out for my hand over the table. "We should talk," he said quietly. "Last night—"

I pulled my hand away from his and grabbed the platter with the eggs. "More eggs?"

Li Wei snatched the eggs from me, and Li Qiang hid an amused smile behind his hand. "After breakfast, Ivy and I have to talk in private," he told his brother. I squirmed in my seat. "You put on your headphones and do not disturb us, you hear?" Li Wei nodded, too busy munching on a piece of charred bacon to pay close attention.

After cleaning the kitchen, Li Qiang held my hand and pulled me inside the room. His brother was already fully invested in a game, and there was no avoiding it any longer. My mouth was a desert, and my heart threatened to explode out of my chest. My sweet intern closed the door behind him and smiled at me. I smiled back however weakly. We had already seen each other naked, so why was I so nervous?

Slowly he approached, that sexy smile of his burning a hole in my heart and making certain parts of my body liquefied. As soon as he was at arm's length, he drew me into a hug, one arm hooked around my waist, the other behind my shoulders.

"Thank you," he whispered, planting a butterfly kiss on my forehead. "Thank you for holding Wei're's hand until he fell asleep and listening to my story of woe when…" He let it hang for a heartbeat. "When I should have been the one showering you with love instead."

I blushed again, that citrusy scent of his awakening a new feeling—not sexual, not completely at least. More. That was the only word I could find to describe what my heart was filling with; so much more than the sensual pleasure his very presence incited in me. "Are you kidding me, Xiǎoli? You have put your dating life on hold to pretend being the boyfriend of a much older woman. I should be thanking you."

Li Qiang's smile widened. "*Shǎ gūniáng.*" I arched an eyebrow. "Why do you always refer to yourself as an old woman? How old are you anyway? Thirty, thirty-one?"

I snorted. "I wish. Try thirty-six… well, in a few weeks." I was practically middle-aged and expecting to start receiving offers from AARP in the mail any day. As a man, he hadn't even reached his prime. I frowned, annoyed by my own thoughts. These were my father's words, not mine. I hated that he had managed to leave his seeds of insecurity in my brain.

He nuzzled the crook of my neck, and I whimpered. He did that so well. "You are hardly an old woman, *gūniáng*. You're beautiful, vibrant, smart, brilliant even. You have the body of a goddess and the face of an angel." I snorted again, and he pulled away just enough to scowl at me. "Who has made you believe you're not good enough? Tell me your exes' names and I will kick their asses." I chuckled, my hand trailing the strong bone of his jaw. "I do know martial arts, you know."

My eyes widen, and I tilted my head. "Really? What color belt?"

He threw his head back laughing. "Well, my knowledge is all theoretical. My mom made me watch Chinese period movies—you know, the ones with all that martial arts and magic—so I could keep up with my family history and culture. I have never taken classes."

"So what you're saying is that I am also an expert vampire slayer because I have watched every single episode of Buffy at least three times?" He nodded, trying hard not to laugh. "And an expert baker because I watched *The Great British Baking Show* so many times?" He nodded again, his lips curving up at the corners. My mouth stretched into a smile. He was so cute on top of everything else. "You're so full of shit."

The awkwardness and uneasiness of a few minutes before had dissipated. His hand slid down my arm, triggering a wave of shivers everywhere else in my body. "I wish you could see yourself like I see you," he whispered, his lips moving over my earlobe. "I think you are the most beautiful, most fascinating woman I've ever met."

While his lips were trailing kisses alongside my jaw, I chuckled. "And you never considered asking me out before now? I mean, you've been working at the agency for a few months."

"Well, boss, I figured with you being older and more successful than me, my forwardness would be unwelcomed and would possibly freak you out," he said. "Also, I wanted to get to know the real you. People put on a mask when they are dating, mostly showing what they think the other one wants to see. I wanted to have a clear picture of who you really were first."

"What's the verdict, then?" I was just as curious as I was scared of what he may say. He obviously liked me enough, but did that interest go beyond a sexual relationship?

"I have good instincts, it seems like." His hand had found its way under my T-shirt and was drawing circles around the bare skin of my side, mere inches away from my breast. I suppressed a moan. "You're even more amazing than what I had thought at first." He pulled me away from him and met my eyes with an intensity that made me quake. "Ivy, I've fallen in love with you." Had I heard that correctly? I blinked rapidly, speechless. "I love you, *gūniáng*. I want our fake relationship to be a real one."

♥ ♥ ♥

"Someone's at the door." Li Wei's screeching didn't quite register right away. All my senses had homed in on Li Qiang's lips and eyes, and the only thing I could hear were his words, his confession. "You told me not to open the door on my own," Wei're yelled again, and my brain finally registered what he was saying.

"We should answer," Li Qiang's said. His body didn't move, eyes still locked on mine. I nodded, anchored to the spot. The young man yelled again. Li Qiang sighed and dropped his hands. "I'll go see who it is."

As he moved away, the space he had occupied felt cold and lonely, my body missing his warmth, the promise of more to come. I stood against the wall for a couple more heartbeats, too tingly to move. When I had finally gathered my wits, I pushed away from the hard surface and joined the two brothers in the living room. Li Qiang was by the front door next to none other than my best friend.

"Amber Lee, what are you doing here?" I was happy to see her but hated to think of what I was missing because of her.

"When you called in sick this morning, I was

worried. Looking at that black eye, I guess I was right." One look at my burning face, and my friend smiled knowingly. I hated when she did that. "Oops, it seems as I interrupted something. You guys play rough." I followed her glance to my waist. Shit, my sleeping shirt was half stuck in my leggings where my not-so-fake-anymore boyfriend had been caressing me. Heat burned in my cheeks. "So, am I to surmise that your fictional relationship is not so fictional anymore?"

I honestly was not sure. I knew how I felt, I knew what Li Qiang had said, but was it real? Or were we being carried away by the sharing of close quarters and the pressure to look and act as if we were dating? I peeked at him as if expecting him to answer for me.

He smiled. "You could say that," he said, and my legs turned to jelly. "I can honestly say I have fallen hard for our boss." An idiotic, unstoppable smile stretched across my lips. "I'm just not sure yet about how she feels. She keeps reminding me I'm almost ten years younger than her, like I care."

Amber Lee took a couple steps toward me, her amused smile morphing into one of concern. "She can blame her father for that," she said. "He's a vicious snake who keeps reminding her time is running away from her."

I frowned. "Amber Lee! That's my business," I hissed. "I'm not a child." I knew she meant well, but every time she came to my defense like that, all it did was make me feel small and helpless, someone to be pitied and not the strong woman I wanted to be.

Both Li Qiang and Amber Lee stared at me, surprise written all over their faces. My boyfriend was the first one to smile, but my friend was not far behind. "There's my girl," she said, wrapping her arms around one of mine. "You're absolutely right. I need to shut up." I nodded, not totally sure she meant it. "But I still want to know what's going on with you guys, and what's up with the black eye."

I stole a glance toward Li Qiang. "Well, you kind of interrupted that discussion," he said, a wink in my direction. "The black eye is a story that can wait for another day. I was about to ask our boss whether we could date for real."

I stared nervously at Li Wei, but he was still fully into his game and blissfully unaware of what we were saying. What should I say? Should I go with what my heart was telling me or what my brain kept whispering? The first wanted to say yes, but the latter thought our age difference was a major problem. My father's voice echoed in my brain, telling me I was a loser for even considering such a disastrous relationship. Li Qiang was just starting his life, his career, while I had been there, done that. When he was my age, I would be pushing fifty with all of what comes along with it. If guys already have a tendency for wandering eyes even with younger wives, what would he do once the woman beside him in bed was wrinkled and tired? My heart, that part of me that knew Li Qiang better, said he would love me just the same, but my father-influenced mind scolded me for being selfish enough to condemn a young man to be attached by duty to an old woman.

Li Qiang's smile faltered for a moment. "You don't have to answer now, *gūniáng*," he said, smile recovered. "You shouldn't rush into this, Ivy. Take as much time as you want. I'll continue to be your fake boyfriend until the show and maybe you'll have decided by then." He turned his attention to Amber Lee. "Would you like a cup of coffee? I think we still have some charred bacon left over."

Amber Lee turned her twinkling eyes to me. "Mmm, burnt bacon, my favorite. Let's go get some." She ran her eyes over Li Qiang and said, "Cute penguins, by the way." And she pulled me along with her toward the kitchen, conversation forgotten, and decisions postponed for another time.

CHAPTER TWELVE

REACHING THE FIRMAMENT

Amber Lee had finally left after nearly waterboarding us about our relationship for hours, and Wei're had fallen asleep early, exhausted from the night before. After a long day of distractions, Li Qiang and I were finally alone.

"Should we resume our conversation in the room?" Li Qiang sneaked behind me in the kitchen while I washed the last of the dinner dishes. Manual labor seemed helpful at keeping all my whirling thoughts tapped down. I whipped my chin up at him and gasped. He chuckled softly, his hands closing on my hips. "Sorry, didn't mean to startle you."

My body had instantly combusted by that simple touch. I took a moment to catch my breath and then, surprising myself, leaned against him. He was warm and welcoming, my back fitting snuggly against his body. I let out a sigh and closed my eyes. "You didn't scare me, Xiǎoli, not at all."

He bent down to kiss the hollow between my neck and my shoulder, his lips soft and hot on my skin. "All is quiet on the home front," he whispered, his mouth moving over my neck. "We could retreat to my room and—"

I didn't give him the chance to finish. In a move that would have put any ninja to shame, I spun around, knotted my hands behind his neck, and kissed him. Screw the age difference. I wanted Li Qiang, and he wanted me. We were both consenting adults and unattached. What could be so wrong about the two of us together? My initial rather primal seizure of his mouth mellowed out as every fiber of my being softened and melded into the feeling. I pried his lips apart with my tongue and hesitantly sought his. He didn't disappoint; his arms went around my waist and pulled me against him as his tongue worked its magic.

"We should go to the room," Li Qiang whispered breathlessly. I stole a glance at Wei're on the couch sleeping. I nodded, and he closed his hand around mine to lead me to the bedroom. Once inside, he leaned into me, my back against the closed door, and kissed me again. Fiercely. "No interruptions tonight."

I somehow found the strength to snort. "Is that a promise?"

His lips were leaving a trail of kisses along my lower jawbone all the way to my ear. "If Wei're wakes up again today, I'll put him in our bed and we can make love in the bathroom."

I would have laughed, except my heart was beating too fast, making it hard to breathe. He had said *our* bed. Our. It was a little thing and yet so overwhelmingly huge that he thought of that bed I had only shared with him the night before as ours. It meant the world to me because I was falling so hard for him. No, I had already fallen head over heels, wholeheartedly, and irrevocably in love with Li Qiang.

Damn!

Distracted by my own thoughts and the racket my pumping heart was making, I yelped when Li Qiang swept me into his arms and carried me romance-novel style to *our* bed. He laid me down gently as if I might break and caressed me with his warm eyes. "I don't want you to feel uncomfortable, Ivy," he said with such longing in his eyes, my stomach flipped. "I can leave."

I had to smile. Propping myself on my elbows, I sat up just enough to clasp the front of his T-shirt and pull him on top of me. "I will never speak to you again if you leave me now." Heat had invaded every inch of my body, pooling in areas I so wanted him to explore. "I've never been so comfortable with a man as I am with you, Xiǎoli, never."

That was the green light he needed; he set down a condom he had retrieved from a drawer on the nightstand, dropped to my side, and got busy pulling the T-shirt over my head and stripping me of my leggings.

He shed his own clothes until he was gloriously naked, stretched out on his side next to me. My wanton eyes roamed his gorgeous, lean body. He didn't have the shoulders of a body builder, being much slimmer than an iron-pumping man, but his shoulders, chest, and abs were covered in strong, well-defined muscle that made me all oozy inside. I continued my eye-tour down to his Adonis belt and found that I had to touch him. When my fingers fluttered over the hard muscle of his hips to his abs, he quivered.

There was no way to hide his desire, and hot bursts of electricity ran through me. "Take it off," I whispered, nodding toward my bra. I wanted to feel his hands on my sensitive skin, have his lips around my breasts. I wanted him inside me. "Please."

Li Qiang leaned over, and as his hands went around to my back to unlatch the bra, his body touched mine. I moaned. His skin was hot, and I thought I'd explode as his hand brushed over the sides of my body to cup my breast, now bare. I threw my head back on the pillow, arching my body toward his touch as he teased my nipple with his thumb. While he moved his hand down my belly, anticipation made me wiggle and whimper like a child wanting her candy. When his fingers sneaked underneath the top band of my panties, I nearly lost it. Sweetest torture ever.

Sitting up, Li Qiang pulled the cotton panties down my legs and threw them on the floor somewhere before locking his eyes on mine. He smiled. "You're so beautiful, my love."

Oh shit! I couldn't stand it anymore. I sat up, grabbed the condom from the nightstand, unwrapped it and straddled him, my legs knotted behind his back, his arousal hard between us. I wrapped my hand around him as I rolled the prophylactic along his length. It was his turn to moan. When he tried to squeeze a hand between us, I lifted my bottom just enough to allow him access to my folds. Magic. With a yelp of pleasure, I pushed him down on the bed and buried him inside me. People say things like this all the time, but I truly saw stars—beautiful, bright, shooting stars exploding in a spectacle of light over our heads. I pushed my hips lower to fully envelop him, and he met my rocking movements with his own in a crescendo that had me gasping for air.

The heat and pressure inside me threatened to explode when he held on to my hips and stopped me. "Stop, I can't hold it much longer," he breathed out.

I was ready too and didn't want to hold any longer. Bracing myself on his hard chest, I moved my hips faster, undulating like a belly dancer, pushing both of us closer and closer to the edge. Once I reached the peak, there was nowhere else to go, so down I went, spiraling out of control, my skin burning and freezing at the same time, every muscle of my body spasming and sparkling. I no longer saw the stars as I traveled the Milky Way; I *was* a star.

CHAPTER THIRTEEN

THE MONSTER AND ME

"I'm a grown-up woman, and I know what I'm doing." My voice didn't waver, my back straight as a board and a defiant glint in my eyes. "Father, trust me for once. I'm an intelligent, resourceful woman."

"That's my girl," Amber Lee exclaimed from behind me. I whipped around to face her. "Now if you could do the same exact thing with your actual father it would be amazing."

I stuck my tongue out at her, annoyed to be caught rehearsing my speech in front of the mirror. "Well, the mirror does not counterattack with disparaging comments," I said, smoothing down my tunic. "How do I look?"

Amber Lee gave me the once-over before replying, "You look great as usual."

"Classy? Professional?" My father always

commented on my style. I dressed like a bum or a hippie, not like the businesswoman I fancied myself to be. I didn't want to give him any excuses to do that this time. I didn't know what the whole "I need to meet you now" was about, but nothing good ever came from such meetings.

I had put on a simple pair of black palazzo pants and a flowing cream Kurta tunic with off-white, high-heeled sandals. I had bunched up my hair in a top bun held by a pair of chopsticks and had white, open blossom earrings that dangled from my ears in a sparse shower of gold. It had taken me almost three hours to get ready for this lunch. I didn't want anything to go wrong.

"You're going to be late, and then you'll have to listen to him complain about it," my friend said, handing me my handbag. "Let's go."

Li Qiang had offered to go with me, to be the buffer between my father and my fragile ego, but I knew I had to face this alone. Instead, I asked him to take care of something for me, and he had agreed. My mind wandered to the events of the past week and whatever heaviness was pressing down on me dissipated, the memory of our lovemaking exciting and soothing at the same time. I must have blushed because Amber Lee gave me the look—that squinting, risen eyebrow look that spoke volumes of what kind of dirt was going through her mind. I turned my back on her and pretended to fix my hair while I willed myself to cool off.

"Okay, let's go," I finally said, swiveling around again.

Amber Lee had offered to drive me to the restaurant and then wait in the car. When I tried to protest, she waved a hand in front of my face and said, "You can't stop me. I will be handy just in case you need a shoulder to cry on afterward." Which I most likely would need if history served.

My father was already at the usual table, handsome and distinguished in a navy blue suit, his snowy hair perfectly trimmed and coiffed. The man could be a silver fox model if he wanted to. I watched him for a moment before he noticed me. That smile that I always hoped would grace his lips when he saw me never happened. Instead, his lips stretched into a thin line of disapproval. I exhaled deeply and crossed the dining room to the table.

"You're late again." He flipped a white napkin in one hand before draping it over his lap.

I pulled out a chair and sat across from him at the small square table, heart already slipping and dropping inside me. A quick glance at my phone told me I was exactly one minute late but right on time for the usual scolding. In silence, I grabbed the napkin and then the menu, hoping it would shield me from his censoring eyes. The waiter came to take our order, and I absently ordered the first thing I saw on the menu. I wasn't going to eat it anyway, so why bother?

"Why didn't you tell me?" Blunt, commanding,

and bitter as usual.

Despite my wishes not to look at him, I raised my eyes to him in surprise. "What didn't I tell you exactly?" Considering we lived totally separate lives, there was a slew of things I hadn't told him.

"About the TV show." Damn, who had told him? "Davis, from the network, told me over dinner the other night. What the hell are you thinking?"

I was thinking it was none of his business and how I wanted to flee out of that restaurant, but I answered, "What do you mean, Father? It's a smart business opportunity, so I took it. You taught me never to pass on good opportunities." Where was I getting the sass?

My father's eyes bulged, his lips pinched, and brow furrowed. "Are you blaming me for your stupidity?" Ouch. Surprisingly enough, anger was quickly replacing the hurt in my chest. "When has an appearance on a morning show become a good business practice? A stupid, fluffy pseudo-news show that will bring your ridiculous matchmaking business to the public."

I swallowed the ball of fire stuck in my throat. "Isn't that what good advertisement aims at doing? Bringing your business under the spotlight?" I wasn't sure where I was getting the guts to argue with my father or how wise that was, but I couldn't stop. I had worked so hard to establish myself as a businesswoman, and all he could see me as was a common cartoonish matchmaker, a joke. "The more people who know about me and my company, the more business it will bring in."

The waiter showed up at our table with the food and, after a quick look at both of us, left the platters behind and rushed away. "If you owned a respectable business, then yes, great opportunity. But you run an online dating site, a glorified pimping service."

Flaming red blinded me for a second. I lowered my eyes, fighting the urge to get up and leave. "I know what you think of me and my job, and there's nothing I can say or do to change your mind," I said, keeping my voice as still and quiet as possible. "So I'm not going to try. Let's just agree to disagree on this. I'm not changing my mind about it."

With a thump, he dropped his forearms onto the table and scowled. "So, you're going to go in front of a large audience to talk about how many people you have convinced they found their one true love and expose your own shameful relationship to your junior?" Ice ran through my veins. "What? You didn't think I'd find out your so-called boyfriend is your intern? An intern who is ten years younger than you."

"We're both adults. There is nothing inappropriate about our relationship." I hated how I suddenly sounded like a teenager.

"Nothing inappropriate? He works for you, for God's sake." His voice had gone an octave lower, a lion ready to pounce. "If he doesn't get what he wants from you, you'll have a sexual harassment suit on your lap." How could this be my father? This ugly-souled, cruel man with no love in his heart for his own flesh and blood.

"What exactly do you think Li Qiang wants from me? I'm not a rich woman; I don't own a top five company. What can he possibly get from me?" I was stupid even to ask. My father was an expert at finding any sordid possibility in everything, no matter how wholesome and good. "My company is small potatoes. I live in a tiny apartment, don't own any jewels or expensive items, and I drive a Mini Cooper. What can I give him that he couldn't get elsewhere?"

He leaned over, stealing a glance around us. "He's from a minority too. You'll end up with a discrimination suit on your head." Despite what I knew about that man, his words still managed to shock me. "And he's a kid. If you were responsible, you'd realize that at your age, all you're doing is holding back this guy."

Wow, he was going to throw everything but the kitchen sink at me. "We love each other!" The explosion caught me by surprise. Sure, I might as well admit it, I was in love with Li Qiang. But how could I be sure of how he felt? Attraction was obviously strong, but love? Did he love me like he said he did? "Mom was totally different from you, and yet you married her. You must have loved her, right?"

He snorted. "You would think that at your age you'd be less naive," he spat. "Your mother embodied everything I despise in a human being. Yes, she was beautiful, and I did have fun while we were dating, but love? Of course I didn't love her."

Good thing I was sitting because the world had just crashed on me. I had always wondered how my parents had ended up together when they were polar opposites. They say that opposites attract, right? So, I assumed that's what had happened. In all these years, he had never said he loved her, but he also had never mentioned he didn't.

"Don't look so shocked, girl. Did you really think I loved your mother?" Yes, I did. I couldn't understand why, but I did believe that. "We were in the process of getting a divorce when she died."

No, no that couldn't be. My mom had never said anything to me about it. No one did. I shook my head, dizzy and nauseated. "You're lying. Mom never told me—"

Another snort escaped his lips. "The silly woman wanted to protect you. She thought she would wait until all the legal procedures were final and then find a way to break it to you. She made me promise not to tell you." Oh my God. I had lived a life of lies. "After she died, there was no point in bringing it up, so I didn't." How could he sound so cool, so collected while trashing my memories? "I married her because she got pregnant. With parents as powerful in business as hers were, I didn't want to risk their wrath by abandoning their precious daughter. I hoped she would bear me an heir, but she failed me even in that. She gave me a daughter who is an embarrassment."

My chest hurt. Now, the horrible eulogy he had delivered at my mother's funeral and the way he had spoken to her attending family members made a lot more sense. At the time, I had thought it was his way of dealing with grief, that heartless side of him that could not deal with real feelings. But now I knew it had come from his heart—if you can call the cold and bitter organ that kept my father alive a heart. He hated me because I was a walking reminder of his wife, a fact he never failed to mention to me. He hated me as much or more than he had hated my beautiful, creative, and loving mother.

My father was a monster, one I had spent most of my thirty-six years trying to please, hoping that underneath all of that ice there was a nugget of love for me. I had wasted all these years on a monster.

♡ ♡ ♡

The tapping on the door got louder, and after a while, even I couldn't ignore it. It wasn't Amber Lee since she had a key, so who else would be knocking at my door? I had not gone to work or Li Qiang's house after the disastrous meal with my father. Instead, I had Amber Lee drive me home. She knew something had happened, even though I had not broken down in tears the whole drive home. But I also had not said a word, and my friend knew me well; I needed time to process everything Father had told me and how I felt about it.

She had dropped me at home after making me promise I would call her when I was ready to talk. Or cry.

I had not shed a tear. In fact, I was not sure how I felt. There was something heavy sitting on my chest, and my jaws hurt from clenching my teeth so tightly, but I couldn't identify my feelings. There were so many, all entangled in a big ball of emotions that I hadn't been able to unravel.

The knocking continued, gentle but insistent. I slowly slid off the couch where I had been sitting for the past two or three hours and walked across the apartment to go see who was at the door. A quick peek through the peephole told me it was my not-so-fake boyfriend. His beautiful face was marred by worry, and my breathing eased a smidgen.

"Go home, Xiǎoli," I said, my forehead against the door. "I'll call you later."

"No way. Open this door, Ivy, please," he said, knocking again. "Don't shut me out. You don't have to talk if you don't want to, but let me sit by you, let me hold you, make you coffee, whatever."

I hesitated. It wasn't as if I didn't want him around; I just didn't want to soil him with the mire of feelings churning inside me, the darkness my father had gifted me. In the end, my need for him won; I opened the door and allowed him to draw me in and envelop me with his strong arms. I hid my face on his chest, smelling the fresh scent of his laundry detergent and the unique lemony scent that was all Li Qiang. He closed the door behind us and led me to the couch, never once pulling apart from me.

"I'm here, *gūniáng*. I'm here for you." I inhaled his scent and allowed myself to sink deeper into his embrace. His arms were a safe space, a place where I felt loved and wanted. I wanted to stay there forever. He didn't move, and I didn't say anything.

I don't know how long we stayed like that, but I may have dozed off for a bit. Eventually I pulled apart a bit to look up at his lovely face. I tried to smile, but it didn't quite work out that way. "He hates me," I said, my voice raspy and shaking. "My father hates me."

He studied my eyes, took a deep breath, and pulled me into his arms again, and the tears that had been delayed for hours erupted in a cascade down my face, soaking his shirt. He didn't say anything, rocking me gently like a baby and peppering the top of my head with kisses. I didn't know I had that many tears in me, but I cried until my eyes hurt and swelled and my nose and my throat were sore. When the sobs began to finally subside, Li Qiang offered to make me coffee.

"I'm a girl. When female hearts break, only chocolate ice cream can save the day," I said, hiccups punctuating my words. "There is some in the freezer."

Li Qiang smiled and brushed his fingers down my cheek before getting up and rushing to the kitchen for the ice cream. A few minutes later, he was back, two bowls in his hands. "No whipped cream," he said apologetically. He handed me one of the bowls and then sat down with the other. "I figure, might as well join you." His sheepish grin made me smile. God, he was adorable.

I slurped the partially melted ice cream, bouncing my glances from the sweetness in the bowl to the sweetness in Li Qiang's eyes and smile. When had I gotten so lucky to get such a wonderful boyfriend— an accidental one at that? With tears still streaking my face, I hiccupped again and said, "I'm sorry you had to see my ugly crying. My father is an expert at bringing out the worst in me." Even as I said it, I knew I had no one to blame but myself. I had allowed him to turn me into this self-doubting, pitiful excuse for a woman because I thought I could make him love me. How naive was I?

"Don't get mad at me," he said, dropping the spoon in the bowl, "but why do you try so hard to please a man who obviously cannot be pleased?"

Sniffling a little, I spooned another large dose of soupy ice cream into my mouth, giving myself time to answer. In the end, I went with the truth. "He's my father. I wanted him to be proud of me. I don't have a mom or siblings—in fact, I have no family. My maternal grandparents died when I was still in elementary school, and my father's family stays well away from us. They live in Malibu and travel all year. I think I've seen them maybe a handful of times my whole life." I sniffled again. "I guess that's why my father is the way he is."

He set the bowl on the cocktail table and looked me in the eye. "Good thing you don't take after them," he said, a smile pulling on the corners of his lips. "You are the most amazing woman I've ever met." I opened my mouth to protest, but he stuck two fingers to my lips. "I don't say this just because I'm hoping for a repeat of two days ago." Cheeky monkey. "I really mean it. From the heart."

I let out a loud sigh. Anger and hurt ebbing out of me, I set my bowl down on the floor and held his hands. "Sorry, my hands are sticky." I giggled nervously. He only held them tighter. "You are not too bad yourself, my sweet intern."

He laughed and gave my hands a little tug. "After my performance in bed—which you have to admit was impressive—you must call me *Bìxià,* not intern."

I raised an eyebrow. "What the hell does that mean?" His mischievous smile spoke volumes.

"Your Majesty," he said in a whisper laced with laughter. "Do I deserve it or not?"

Even though I was still hiccupping leftover sobs, my heart felt so much lighter, and I couldn't help it, I burst out laughing at the silliness of his comment. Before I knew it, I opened my mouth and blurted out, "I love you, *Bìxià.*" As soon as it was out, I covered my mouth with my free hand. What had I just done?

A moment of silence stretched between us—it was as if we had been sucked into the vacuum of outer space. All I could hear was my own heart, banging against my chest and vibrating in my ears. I didn't dare take my eyes off Li Qiang who had gone very quiet and whose smile had vanished, his hand still grasping mine.

After what felt like an eternity, he leaned over and placed a slow, gentle kiss on my lips. He pulled away far enough for my eyes to be able to focus on his clearly and then smiled. "I love you too, *gūniáng*," he said. "I love you so much."

CHAPTER FOURTEEN

A SHOULDER TO CRY ON

Damn neighbors are playing music too loud again. I tried to ignore the buzzing and the high notes of violin, hoping it would stop. It didn't. Annoyed, I opened my eyes and licked my dry lips. Wow, my eyes were sore. I rubbed them with the back of my hand to clear the blurriness but only made it worse. Why did my eyes and the corners of my nose burn? Reality hit me all at once; I had cried my eyes out in the arms of my sweet boyfriend and—holy shit! We had both uttered the three magic words, right?

Suddenly aware of a heartbeat beneath my ear, I pushed myself up slightly to glance at Li Qiang, fast asleep on the couch, one leg hanging over the edge and a hand still holding mine. We had both fallen asleep, me tucked between him and the back of the couch, half draped over him. I stared at his face in something like awe; he was beautiful, or at least I thought so. His eyes were closed in perfect crescents, edged in jet-black eyelashes, the bruise from a week ago faded into almost nothing, and his full lips relaxed into a peaceful half smile.

Li Qiang loved me. My fake boyfriend was in love with me. A good man—honest, sweet, and supportive—had fallen for the flawed, never-good-enough me. Was that even possible? I had always hoped so, but reality had taught me otherwise. None of my boyfriends in the past had stuck around for long, I had a knack to disappoint the men around me one way or another; I was too boring, too short, not busty enough, not pretty enough, too busy, too everything or not enough. I couldn't even make my own father love me; how did I expect to conquer a lover's heart?

"Stop it." Li Qiang's words startled me. He opened his eyes and sought mine. "Whatever you're labeling yourself with, it's not true, so stop it."

Could he read minds? "I wasn't thinking anything," I lied with a pitiful attempt at a smile.

He let go of my hand and cupped my cheek. "Every time you are putting yourself down, you get a look," he said softly. "Why can't you believe how amazing you are?"

He was too sweet. "Because I want to hear you say it," I quipped, trying to steer the conversation away from my lack of self-confidence. I plopped a brief kiss on his lips. "You taste good."

A sunny smile stretched his lips. "Like a cupcake?" He twirled a lock of my messy hair with his finger.

"More like Belgian dark chocolate." The truth was I would never be able to describe his taste other than as uniquely his. "My favorite."

He pulled me in for another kiss, longer and hungrier. "I guess we should thank Teresa," he said, a bit breathless. "If it wasn't for her insistence in this living-together thing, we might never—" I shut him up with another kiss, my mouth devouring his. I pressed my tongue between his lips and caressed his. His taste *was* intoxicating, and heat pooled in my girly parts and beyond. He suckled on my lower lip before whispering, "Wei're is not here right now. We could—"

Bracing myself with my hands on his chest, I pulled myself upward and away from him. "Shit! Wei're! He's alone." How could we have forgotten the kid?

Li Qiang laughed and pulled me down on him again. "First, ouch! You just crushed my chest," he said, planting another kiss on my chin. "Second, I'm crazy about you, but he is still my little brother; I wouldn't leave him alone. Amber Lee is with him."

I breathed out a sigh of relief. My best friend had come through for me again. "We could take a bath together then," I suggested, surprising myself. "I have a garden bathtub." That tub was in part what had sold me this condo. The apartment was nothing special, but it had a nice-size main bathroom and a lovely small balcony with a view to the park. He wagged his eyebrows. I chuckled. "Is that a yes?"

"No, it's a hell yes." In a smooth move, he grabbed my waist and got us both on our feet. "Let's go fill that tub right now." He wiggled his brows again. "I have a mental list of things I want to try on you."

I swatted him playfully. "Good luck with that." My wide smile belied my words. "I'll go fill the tub; you make us some coffee."

The bathtub was only halfway full when he showed up in the bathroom, two mugs of hot chocolate in his hands. "You said you love dark chocolate, and I found this mix in your pantry. I figured why not? Chocolate is sexier than coffee, right?"

I took the mug from his hands and sniffed it. It smelled heavenly. I had bought that mix a couple months ago to treat myself for a successful match of two of my customers but had never gotten around to drink it. Too busy, too blah…. To interrupt my thoughts, I took a long gulp of the sweet brew. The warmth slid easily down my throat, liquid comfort for my troubled soul.

Li Qiang put his mug down and covered my hands with his, my cup still between mine. "You're having those thoughts again, aren't you?" Was there such a thing as a mind-hack firewall? He could read me too well. He took the hot chocolate away from me and set it by his, and then he held my hands up to his lips and kissed them. "I want to show you how amazing I think you are, how beautiful and sexy, how smart and warm...." With a gentle pull, he had me within his arms. "I love you, Ivy, love everything that you are, the good and the bad. I wish I could make you believe that."

I wanted to believe it; I guess at some level I did believe it. When he kissed or touched me, I felt beautiful, stunning, bright like a star in the sky. "I love you too, Xiǎoli."

He dropped my hands, turned to the bathtub to turn off the running water, and smiled at me. The air was rich with the fragrance of lavender and chamomile as the waves of heat wafted from the tub. Li Qiang began unbuttoning his shirt, now stained with mascara from my tears, but I stopped him. I wanted to be the one doing it. I pulled the parts of his shirt that were still tucked in his pants and began working on the buttons. Then I slid it off him with a growl of impatience.

He chuckled. "Patience, sweetheart," he said, playing with the ties of my sweatpants. "I'm going to show you just how amazing I think you are."

And he sure did.

♥ ♥ ♥

Amber Lee had called twice, threatening to drop Wei're in the nearest orphanage if we didn't come home soon. We chose to ignore her. There was plenty of food and entertainment in Li Qiang's apartment to keep her and the boy for weeks, and I knew my friend was just dying to know what had happened. Taking total advantage of being alone for the first time in a while, my boyfriend and I lingered in bed, making love or just talking while sipping coffee and hot cocoa. My body had never felt so alive. Li Qiang's hands and lips had awakened every cell in my being, and I felt like a live wire, buzzing with pleasure and excitement. Under his tender love and care, I could almost believe I was indeed the superstar he thought I was.

It was already dark by the time we finally decided we should give Amber Lee a break. We got dressed, called an Uber, and returned to Li Qiang's place. The world around us had slowed and quieted down—or so it seemed. My senses were tuned only to my man's scent, his beautiful eyes and lips, the way his skin and his hard muscles felt under my touch; everything else was muted and blurred. I only half heard the brief conversation he had with the driver before we left the car and was barely aware of it driving away as we stood on the sidewalk, hand in hand. Love was really a drug, wasn't it? And I was flying high on it.

I was surprised when Wei're came running to us, so into my own head I hadn't noticed we had arrived home. The boy hugged me as if he hadn't seen me in ages, and finally awake, I hugged him back. "Goodness, Wei're. You saw me this morning."

"I thought your father had killed you or something," the young boy said. I threw a dagger look at Amber Lee, who lowered her eyes in shame. She had mentioned my father to Li Wei. I would have to kill her later.

My father was not a subject I shared with everybody. "Amber Lee said he's the devil."

I huffed. "Amber Lee says a lot of things she shouldn't. My father is not the nicest person in the world, but he would never kill me." At least, I hoped not. After today's conversation, I wasn't so sure anymore.

Li Qiang, who had let go of my hand, ruffled his brother's thick hair. "Let my girlfriend go, brat. You're going to suffocate her."

Wei're let go of me, smiled, and took off to his usual spot by the window. "I'm glad you're alive," he yelled out. "So I can go back to my game in peace."

I chuckled and reached out for my boyfriend's hand again. I was not comfortable not touching him for long. "So, Amber Lee…." I let that hang, and it worked; my friend looked as if she would gladly crawl into a hole if she could find one handy.

"I only mentioned your father in passing," she said, her eyes avoiding mine. "He has a fertile imagination and made up this whole *Criminal Minds*-type story." She was a lost cause, so I laughed, shaking my head. She perked up. "So how was the time alone?" she asked in a singsong voice. "Got a lot done?" Her eyes were as round as saucers. Wicked woman. "Well?"

"I could use another coffee," I suggested to Li Qiang, who immediately took off to the kitchen. I stepped closer to my friend, hooked my arm through hers, and whispered conspiratorially, "Yes, we got a lot done, like you put it." She got animated, turning halfway toward me. "But damned if I tell you any of it."

With a huff of disappointment, Amber Lee stomped a foot. "Really? You're not going to tell your bestie how delicious your handsome guy was? How selfish."

A chuckle bubbled out of me. "He *is* delicious, but that's all I'm going to say." Mostly because I wouldn't know how to describe how he made me feel; it went beyond physical pleasure into another dimension of reality. I would never be able to find the words to describe it.

Li Qiang came back with two cups of coffee and an amused twitch on his lips. "I guess you figured out that we are no longer a fake couple, right?" he said, handing one of the cups to my friend.

Amber Lee shook her head and then almost dropped her mug. "Fuck, almost forgot," she said. "They've called from the studio. The show is going live this coming Sunday. She said she'll email you the details."

My heart dropped a few inches. Even though I didn't have to worry about lying on the show anymore, the thought of being on TV was nerve-racking. With all that had happened since then, I had almost forgotten it was coming.

Unlike me, Li Qiang didn't look worried. "Finally," he said. "Then we can put this whole thing behind us."

Those few words fell like rocks in my stomach. What did he mean? Put what behind us? Our relationship or just the show? All the insecurities he had managed to erase with his loving came back with a vengeance. I knew I wasn't good enough to hold him, to deserve his loyalty and love. I knew it. My father was right; I was just not good enough.

"I have a headache," I murmured, my eyes on the floor. "I think I'm going to bed, guys. Good night." Before they could protest, I spun on my heels and rushed to the room. I didn't undress; I threw myself in bed, buried my face on the pillow, and cried. It was just a matter of time before I lost Li Qiang.

CHAPTER FIFTEEN

ON STAGE

It was the second time I visited the ladies' room inside the TV studio. Thankfully, no one was there to witness my dry heaving in the stall, my stomach determined to empty itself of whatever was left in it. Since I hadn't eaten since the day before, all I could puke out was foul air. I was a mess of nerves and frustration. If my father could see me, he'd have a field day. I could hear him as clearly as if he was standing beside me. *"No backbone. You're an embarrassment to you and me. You thought you could handle it, didn't you? I could have told you, you couldn't. You're a failure. A nothing."* A new wave of nausea worked its way through me.

I hadn't seen Li Qiang since the day in his condo. Being the gentleman that he was, my boyfriend didn't question me when, the next day, I told him I wanted to stay at my place until the day of the show. I needed to clear my mind and do some work, and being around him distracted me to no end. However true that last statement was, the whole truth was I was terrified. Despite my heart telling me I was full of shit, my inner critic wouldn't shut up; once the show was over, Li Qiang was going to dump me and move on to bigger and better ventures. My young boyfriend would find someone as young as he was who was prettier, bustier, better in bed than I was…. The list went on forever, and despite my rebel side fighting against those poisoned bullets, the inner critic was winning. My father was winning.

"Ms. Tower," a high, female voice said from behind the closed door. "It's almost time. We need to touch up your makeup."

I took a deep breath, pulled a long section of toilet paper and wiped my mouth with it. "Coming," I managed to squeak out. I straightened myself up, turned around, and opened the door, hoping I had nothing nasty on my face. A tall, skinny woman with large, round glasses was waiting for me. "I hope I'm not a fright."

She smiled kindly, waving the large makeup brush in her hand. "Don't worry. Nothing that can't be fixed," she said, gesturing me to come closer. "You're not the only one who lets her nerves get the best of her." She chuckled and examined my face like a surgeon inspecting her patient. "You have a beautiful face with lovely brown eyes and great skin tone. And those freckles!"

I flinched. "Me?" Maybe there was a good reason for her glasses after all. "I'm such a plain Jane." Shit! Why was I repeating my father's old nickname for me? I hated it when he said that, and here I was saying the same thing.

The woman furrowed her brow and pushed her glasses up the bridge of her nose with one finger. "Plain? You gotta be kidding, right? I would kill to have those eyes, and your skin? It's smooth and youthful with just enough texture to it not to make you look like a doll." I almost laughed. I had never heard my old acne scars called texture. "You barely need any makeup. How old are you anyway? Twenty-five?"

I snorted, some of the tension from a moment ago forgotten. "I'm thirty-six—or will be very soon. Stop flattering me, Miss"—I read the name of her badge— "Kay."

Kay's lips stretched into a sunny smile. "I don't flatter; I tell the truth," she said, waving her brush in the air again like a maestro. "People have a tendency to be blind to their own beauty. Let's go to your dressing room and get you ready before Teresa has one of her conniption fits, shall we?"

Feeling lighter, I followed her to the nearby dressing room. Weird how those words from a stranger had made me feel so much better. Foolish of me of course to listen to my inner critic. I was an adult, a successful adult at that; why did I still react to my father's words?

Not wasting any time, Kay had me ready to go in a blink of an eye. After scanning my face one last time, she crossed her arms, smiled, and declared, "Masterpiece. Easy when you have a great canvas to work on." I couldn't help it; I drew her to me in a bear hug. "Don't mess up the makeup," she yelped. I let her go, and she shook her head, a tiny smile dancing in the corner of her lips. "Silly woman, you almost ruined the work of art." She shooed me out of the room, clucking as if I was a chicken. "Go. Your gorgeous boyfriend is waiting by the set."

My gorgeous boyfriend! Li Qiang, the wonderful man I loved and whom I had practically ignored for the past few days. Guilt and apprehension filled me. He didn't deserve this. Even if I was right and he'd be gone from my life after the show, he had been my anchor for the past few weeks. He deserved more from me, so much more. I couldn't let my father win this time. I couldn't.

I lifted my head and followed the signs to the set. As soon as I turned the corner, my eyes locked with Li Qiang's, who was leaning on the wall, arms crossed and brows wrinkled. When he saw me, he uncrossed his arms and pushed himself away from the wall. I swallowed, a mixture of joy and fear swelling in my heart as I walked toward him.

"Are you okay? You didn't answer any of my calls or texts." The frantic tone in his voice was telling of how worried he had been. Guilt stabbed me harder.

"What's wrong?"

His long arms went around me and tightened in a hug. "Sorry, Xiǎoli. I'm fine. I just needed to sort some things in my head," I said, hating the ridiculousness in my words. What did I have to sort out? The fact that I had a beautiful, sweet, and amazing man who claimed he loved me? One I loved with all my heart. Or the fact that my insecurities kept hounding and filling me with scenarios of a future that may never come to pass? "I'm so sorry."

He planted a kiss on the crook of my neck, and my skin tingled in pleasure. "I understand. We all have our demons to deal with from time to time. Mine still rear their ugly heads once in a while." The accident that had hurt Li Wei so seriously and almost killed both of them. Right, he did understand about having things that haunt your life; he still didn't drive because of it. "I just want you to know you can always come and talk to me. Any time of day or night. Got it?"

I nodded, unable to say anything. He said that now, but would he still say the same after this whole promotional thing was over? *Father, get out of my head!*

An older man with headphones and a clipboard stepped in from the set. "We're ready for you," he said. "We're going live in five."

For better or worse, this was it. We were on.

❤ ❤ ❤

I was sweating even before the cameras were rolling. Beads of perspiration collected on my forehead and between my breasts as I stared at the small crowd around us—cameramen, makeup artists, gophers, and other people I had no idea what their job titles were. The set was deceptively intimate with a stuffed armchair, a matching love seat, and a small cocktail table where a staff member had placed three coffee mugs displaying the TV station logo. This setup should have made me more comfortable, but instead, it made me even more nervous; the red of the upholstery and the soft rug beneath our feet together with the bright lights and the frantic movement around us triggered a full-on sensory overload. I wanted to stuff my ears, shut my eyes tightly, and go lock myself in the nearest empty room. Why had I agreed to do this?

"Are you ready?" Teresa sat on the armchair to our left, not a hair out of place and perfectly made-up. Bile rose in my throat and panic rolled inside my stomach. "This is going to be great." *Speak for yourself. I might barf.*

Li Qiang, sitting next to me, placed a warm hand on my thigh. The heat ignored the barrier of the material of my dress and seeped through skin and muscle, directly into my veins. I sighed, some of the stress dissipating under his touch. "It will be okay, *gūniáng*," he whispered, leaning in slightly. "Remember that you are amazing and that I love you." His voice, his words had the effect of a full-body warm wrap; every muscle in my body relaxed.

I scooted closer to him, wanting to absorb more of his comforting warmth as he draped an arm over my shoulders. I'm sure we looked like a real couple, which of course we were now, the pleased smile on Teresa's lips confirming that fact.

There was a sudden frenzy of movement and voices, and everything went silent. We were on the air. Li Qiang squeezed my leg again, and I let out the air I was holding in.

"Welcome to the Early Morning Show," Teresa started, her back straight as a rod and her plastic smile firmly etched on her face. "I'm your hostess, Teresa Lord, and with me I have a local entrepreneur and her fiancé." She turned her head to us and smiled even wider, her perfect teeth blinding under the stage lights. "Welcome to our show, Ms. Tower and Mr. Li."

What should I do? Should I turn to the camera and say hello? Li Qiang saved me from having to decide, and I mimicked him as he waved and smiled in the direction of the camera.

Teresa turned away from us again. "Ms. Tower is a local woman who has opened and manages a very successful dating agency here in our own town." Her eyes swung to me. "Could you tell our audience, Ms. Tower, what makes your business different from other dating places and why, in your opinion, is it as successful as it is?"

Surprising even myself, I swallowed the nervous

knot in my throat and began. "Well, Ms. Lord, in my agency, The Ivory Tower, we pride ourselves on personal customer service. Each and every one of our clients receives personal and customized service." The more I said, the more relaxed I felt. Falling into my usual business demeanor, I managed to forget the cameras and the idea that thousands of people would be watching the show. For that moment, it was just me talking to a perspective client or sponsor, something I had done a million times.

I spoke for a while about how the business was run, what kind of services we provided, and what we had planned for the future. The studio interspersed our talking with short testimonials from past and present clients, some of which were now either married or in successful relationships. Their obvious satisfaction with The Ivory Tower agency made my heart swell with pride. This was my doing, my brain baby, and I should never allow my father or anyone to demean it.

When Teresa changed the subject from the business to my personal life, I was startled. Talking about business was one thing I was very comfortable doing; speaking of my love life was not.

"Obviously, you live what you preach, Ms. Tower," Teresa was saying. "You have found the love of your life right where you both work, correct?"

I nodded stupidly, all my words diluted into nothing. Li Qiang came to my rescue. "Yes, I am an intern in Ivory's agency."

Teresa chuckled, her laughter coming across as plastic as her smile. "So, technically you work for her." Uh-oh, that sounded bad. Was she trying to suggest something insidious was going on?

Li Qiang shrugged it off. "I guess so, but the truth is I took this job because I wanted to get close to her." I whipped my head around to look at him. What? How come he had never said anything? He brushed a finger on my cheek and continued. "I had met her at a job fair—she probably can't remember it because she was busy and we only exchanged a couple words. I was bewitched by the way she took care of everyone who addressed her, with kindness and genuine interest." He smiled at me while I gaped like a fish out of water. "I watched from across the room for hours and made a decision right then and there that I was going to get to know her better."

Teresa clapped her hands. "That is so romantic," she exclaimed. "Then what happened?"

"Instead of taking the job I got offered—a real job with benefits—I decided to do an internship for Ivory Towers," my wonderful—and apparently sneaky— boyfriend said, his hand closing gently on my shoulder. "I thought that maybe I would lose interest in her, but my interest and admiration just grew with each day. Mind you, Ivory didn't seem to even notice I was there beyond my work."

I laughed, a little choked with it all. He had been interested in me that long? Way before I dared to even look at him as more than just a cute guy who worked for me. I had no idea. "You never told me that," I whispered, not sure I wanted to share that information with the public at large. He nodded, and my face turned into a boiling mess.

Teresa opened her mouth to ask something, but Li Qiang cut her off. "I fell in love with her and asked her out. I was a little nervous that she'd say no because of our professional relationship, but I won't be the intern for long, and it's hard enough to find someone you truly click with, isn't it? It'd be dumb not to pursue it."

Teresa nodded emphatically. She was eating it up, but then again, so was I. Was he speaking from the heart, or was it all part of the plan to make the world believe in us as a couple? He had changed the story, the one we had rehearsed a thousand times, so I wanted to believe this was so much more than a tale to impress the audience.

My father would say I was being a stupid fool.

Teresa stared at the camera for a heartbeat, a slow, intentional smile stretching her lips. "You, Mr. Li, are an award-winning author. Will your love story appear in one of your future releases?"

"I don't write romance, but I know that what I feel in my heart for this woman will most definitely seep into each and every one of my stories from now on." Li Qiang turned face on to the cameras and declared, "I want the whole wide world to know that I love this woman and that I will give her my whole body and soul, if she'll accept me. I want to spend the rest of my life getting to know and making Ivory the happiest woman in the world."

My father could go suck a lemon!

CHAPTER SIXTEEN

LOVES ME NOT

"What shall we do to celebrate?" Amber Lee was far more excited than I was about putting the whole TV thing behind us and had been waiting for us outside the studio. "I'm paying."

Li Qiang, still holding my hand, laughed. "In that case, we should go for lobster and champagne. What do you think, sweetheart?"

A wide, unrelenting smile had been plastered on my lips since my boyfriend had declared his love for me in front of the cameras. I nodded. "Since it's barely seven in the morning, we probably should stick to coffee and pancakes."

He pulled me in for one-arm hug. "See? If it wasn't for you and your wisdom, I'd be drunk out of my freaking mind by nine in the morning." He chuckled. "Amber Lee, you pick the breakfast place."

My best friend, a self-proclaimed foodie, steered us down the block into a sleepy twenty-four-hour diner she swore had the best waffles in town. At that time on Sunday morning, the only people in the restaurant were the staff and a few stragglers who had either not gone to bed yet or wanted to get their fill of quiet. We slid into a booth and scooped the menus from the holder. The server, a woman probably in her forties, took our order and walked away, leaving us to ourselves.

"You guys did great," Amber Lee said. "I watched the whole thing on my phone while I sat in the car. I just know that the whole town is going to fall for you two lovebirds. That declaration of love, Li Qiang, had me all hot and bothered."

Our hands had found each other again between us on the seat. "I'm glad this is all over and we can go on with our normal lives." I went stiff. What did he mean? Had the whole speech been just an act? Was I really that naive and love starved that I couldn't see through the pretense? "I was afraid Teresa would find something to hang over our heads, but it looks as if everything went swimmingly." Pretending I needed my hand to sip my coffee, I pulled it away from his. Li Qiang threw me a brief look but didn't look fazed.

My empty stomach was once again threatening to empty itself further as a boulder the size of the Empire State Building took residence there. The tension inside my chest grew, and hot tears pooled in my eyes. I couldn't cry. I wouldn't give anyone the satisfaction of knowing what a fool I was. Why had I believed I had finally met a man who loved and respected me for who I was—someone who didn't see me as the weak failure my father had always told me I was?

I needed to get out of there, but I was stuck between my oh-so-fake boyfriend and the wall, so I lowered my eyes and pretended I was invisible; better to be unseen than seen as a loser. The toxic fumes of betrayal suffocated me. "I need to go to the bathroom," I said, hoping the pain didn't taint my voice.

Li Qiang, still engrossed in conversation with Amber Lee, stood up and let me slide past him. I didn't wait around to see if anyone noticed I was gone and dashed through the small diner into the restrooms. Thankfully, there was no one there to hear my sobbing. I sat on the toilet, stall door locked, and cried my eyes out, face hidden in my hands. Unwisely and against all odds, I had fallen in love with my intern. I had been so flattered by his kindness and attention, I forgot we were putting on an act. Yes, it had gotten physical and certain words might even have been exchanged, but, damn, I was an adult, I should have known better than just to assume his feelings for me went beyond a physical attraction. Foolishly, I had wanted—needed— to believe he loved me the way I had always wanted to be loved.

My phone vibrated in my pocket. I wiped my tears with the back of my hand and pulled it out. My father! Before I could stop myself, I pressed *talk*. "Father?" I hoped he couldn't hear the tears in my voice.

"Are you happy now?" The usual gruff, accusatory tone. Muddled by my sadness, I had no idea what he was talking about. I waited. "Are you proud of yourself to have that—that… *immigrant* have his paws all over you on TV?" The word "immigrant" was spat out with so much disdain I could almost taste its acrid flavor. "It was bad enough to show up in front of a large audience and boast about your silly dating services, but to have that Asian child fawn all over you in public…. How could you, Ivory? How could you embarrass me that way?"

It took me a few seconds to process what he was saying. My head was not in the right place, as if I was watching myself from far away. I couldn't speak.

"Ivory Tower, answer me!"

The image of a much younger me cowering in front of my father's desk, shaking from head to toe as I was severely admonished for something so trivial even my childish mind couldn't understand. He had never laid a hand on me. Never. But his words had always been as sharp as a surgeon's scalpel and just as life changing. Those words had shaped the way I viewed myself and how I perceived the way others saw me. What did he want me to say? That he was right, that I was an embarrassment to him and myself? That Li Qiang was not worthy of a Tower because of his age or ethnic background? That my hard-earned professional success was worthless?

"Answer me, young lady." The poison in his words slid off me this time. I was too upset, too heartbroken already. No one could break something that was already shattered into a million tiny pieces.

I stared at the screen for a moment and then pressed *end*. Before I slipped the phone back in my pocket, I turned it off. I stood up, smoothed my dress with my hands, and left the stall. The eyes looking back at me in the bathroom mirror were not familiar anymore. Something inside me had shifted. I just wasn't sure whether for better or worse.

❤ ❤ ❤

"Why are you packing?" Wei're asked, hovering over me like a tyke over candy. He had been following me around all morning, forgoing playing his favorite games and doing his schoolwork, which was weird enough without having him behind me every time I turned around. I had tripped over him several times already as I moved about the house picking up my things to take home.

"I've told you already; we only moved in together because of this TV show," I said for the third time, rolling my nightshirt and leggings into a disorganized bundle and stuffing them into the already burgeoning suitcase. "Now that's done, we can move back to our original places."

Li Wei did this funny nose thing he did—he called it the piglet snort—and continued. "But you guys are dating. Why live apart?"

Sighing, I ran the palm of my hand over my face and sat on the edge of the bed before patting the spot beside me. "Sit, Wei're. Just because we're dating doesn't mean we have to live together," I said, my words sounding as fake as the so-called diamond ring one of my preschool friends had given me. "We have our own places, and it's kind of stupid to be paying for two condos and live in one."

The boy shook his head, squinting his narrow eyes into a mere slit. "Something smells rotten." I opened my mouth, but he stopped me. "And it's not because I haven't showered today." He was getting to know me a little too well if he could guess my comebacks. "Why don't you get married and sell one of your condos? My mom says you should. She really likes you."

My heart did a sad little tap dance. "I really like her too, Wei're." I did. I liked the whole family. They were so much closer to what I had always envisioned a family to be than mine. They bickered all the time, but their love for one another was obvious in the way they looked at each other, the things they said, the willingness to be there any time they were needed.

My father, my only remaining family, had been calling me several times a day since that one-sided phone conversation the day before. I spent that whole day at work, making up tasks that didn't exist and hiding from Li Qiang. In the evening, I invited myself to Amber Lee's place for a girls' night in, and this morning, I waited until Li Qiang was out on a job run to come to his condo and collect my things. My friend had been very curious, but in the end, I think she bought my I-need-a-girlfriend break excuse.

"Grown-ups are so complicated," Li Wei concluded, playing with a pair of my socks. "Are these zebras?"

I snatched the zebra socks from his hands with a chuckle. "Stop being so nosy, Wei're." I was going to miss the little brat. "Funny how your chickenpox never really bloomed, don't you think?" I threw him a sideway glance, watching for a reaction.

His eyes rounded, and he stuttered for a moment. "I… I was just following orders." I laughed, and he slumped his shoulders. "Stop teasing me. You know it was my mom who made it up. She wanted to find out whether you guys were really dating."

I put the socks I had rolled into a ball in the suitcase. "I know, I'm just messing with you." I enjoyed watching him squirm. "Why would we pretend to be dating anyway?" Granted, we were, but it was for such an off-the-wall reason there was no way his mom would have suspected.

Li Wei sat on the edge of the bed. "Li Qiang is very picky when it comes to girls and has never had a real girlfriend—not the kind you introduce to Mom," he explained. My heart warmed. Sweet Xiǎoli. "My mom kept bugging him about it, so when he told us he was dating and that he was willing to have you meet us and that you worked together, she was suspicious.

She thought he was making something up just to shut her up."

I couldn't help it; I laughed. "Your mom is too funny," I said. "Why has Li Qiang never had a girlfriend?" As beautiful and smart as he was, I couldn't imagine him being celibate. Of course, Wei're hadn't said he didn't date, only that he hadn't had a relationship.

The boy lowered his eyes to his interlaced hands. "I'm not sure, but I think it was because of the accident." The accident with his brother? Why would that affect him that way? "Ever since we almost died in that stupid accident, he's afraid to get attached to anyone." For fear of loss. If you don't have someone you love, losses are easier to handle. Was he afraid to love someone only to lose her like he almost lost his little brother? "He dates but never the same girl twice." Li Wei looked up at me. "Until you. He really loves you, Ivy. You won't break his heart, will you?"

I thought he would be the one breaking my heart. Li Qiang was not as ready to fall in love as his brother thought he was. He had been nice enough to agree to this ridiculous game to save face, but love? How could he love me when I didn't love myself?

"I'd never break his heart, but I'm not sure he loves me like you say he does, Wei're," I told him, hating myself for having this conversation with his brother.

Uncharacteristically, Li Wei blew me a raspberry, spittle sprinkling my face. I wiped it with the back of my hand and made a disgusted sound. "Don't be stupid. Anyone who has seen you together knows my brother is head over heels in love with you. It's pretty pathetic actually and kind of gross." He shuddered as if I had just eaten a bug, but I was too surprised by his words to laugh. Was he right? But Li Qiang had clearly said at the diner that everything had been for the show. I shook my head. No, the young man was mistaken; Li Qiang was just a great actor and a good man, willing to help me in a tight situation.

I ruffled his hair. "Whatever that might be, you need to stop pretending you're sick and go back to school," I told him. "I don't want to be blamed for your lack of education."

He laughed. "Don't worry, my mom takes school very seriously," he said, playing with the fringes on one of my dresses piled up on the suitcase. "What do you think I'm doing when I curl up by the window?"

"Gaming?"

"Wrong!" He looked particularly pleased to catch me in a mistake. "I'm in class. My teacher is a tech wiz, and she has me connected to the class camera so I can attend class without actually being there." My mouth must have fallen open because the little twerp had the nerve to press my chin up with a finger. "See? Never assume you know what's going on."

I wanted to retort with something smart but was left speechless. He had been in school all the time I thought he was playing games online. Color me impressed and confused. "Well, good." Not the best comeback, but it was all I could come up with. "I'm glad you're not neglecting your studies because of a fake illness."

I closed the suitcase and pulled it down from the bed onto the floor. I rolled it to the living room, grabbed my duffel bag, looked around, and took a deep breath. This was it. It was a beautiful dream, but sooner or later we all have to wake up and face reality; the reality was that Li Qiang was an amazing young man with a brilliant future and a kind heart who had taken pity on an older, unloved woman. End of story.

"Well, Wei're, I'm leaving," I told the boy. "You be good and do not open that door for anyone." His brother would be home in less than an hour, and there was food made in the fridge. "If you feel lonely, call your mom to come pick you up since the jig is up." He raised a brow. "It means you can tell your mom we know you're not really sick." I ruffled his hair again. "What are they teaching you in that school anyway?"

I turned to leave but found myself suddenly anchored by a ten-year-old. Wei're had wrapped his skinny arms around my waist and held me tightly. "Don't go, Ivy. I'll miss you." Oh my God, he was going to make me cry. "Please, my brother loves you. Trust me on this."

As much as I wanted to believe him, that was the one thing I couldn't do. There was no way Li Qiang loved me.

CHAPTER SEVENTEEN

SLAY THE BEAST

I corrected the smudge of mascara with the edge of a tissue. It was the third time today that a tear or two escaped my control and rolled down my face to mess up my makeup. I stared at my own pathetic face, slightly blotched from the previous night of crying despite the careful tending that morning before work. I was thankful to have my own office where I could hide from curious eyes behind closed blinds. It hurt too much. After years of protecting my heart by not allowing myself to fall seriously for anyone, I had fallen blindly into Li Qiang's trap. Not that I blamed him. I didn't. I knew his heart was in the right place, but he couldn't have guessed I would truly fall for him.

I flung the soiled tissue into the trash can, sniffled a couple times, and sat back at my desk. There was no doubt in my mind, no work would be accomplished today. Heartache blinded me to everything else. How could I have been so stupid? All my relationships before Li Qiang had been lukewarm and frustrating, but softer on the heart by far. My previous boyfriends had been mostly jerks with no intention of sticking around after a bit of fun. One of them had—unbeknown to me—dated me so he could insinuate himself in my father's inner circle. Another saw me for what I was: a pushover who wanted to believe in people's innate goodness. Needless to say, it didn't end well. After a few months of bending over backwards to make him happy, even my idiot self knew it wasn't working. The one thing all of them had in common was that despite leaving a bitter aftertaste, they did not shatter my heart into the million pieces my fake relationship did.

"Why did you leave?" I was so inside my head I didn't notice Li Qiang coming in and closing the door behind him. "Is everything okay? Wei're said you were acting weird."

I fake laughed, hiding my eyes from him. "I just figured that there was no reason for me to impose on you guys anymore." Oh God, was my voice shaky?

My lovely intern made a beeline to the chair across from mine and sat down, leaning over the desk and covering my hand with his. I trembled. I loved the feel of his skin against mine. "You were not imposing, *gūniáng*," he said in a whisper. "I love having you there. And so does my brother." He chuckled. "I think you might have broken his young heart."

I made a sound that was a cross between a sob and a chuckle. "I love him too, but we both have our lives, and I hate that he wasn't going to school and hanging out with his friends because of me." Partly true. Under the pretense of being infected with chickenpox, Li Wei hadn't left the house for anything. The poor kid must have been going stir-crazy. "This way we are all back to normal." Or what was to be the new normal for me. "You're not mad, are you?"

He shook his head. "No, of course not. I just enjoyed having you all to myself, that's all." *Stop being so sweet!* "Can we have dinner together? Please."

The last thing I wanted to do was torture myself by spending time with the man I loved more than anyone else in the world, but we had to talk things out. There was the "breakup" to plan and other silly details that would end our act. I nodded, choked up by all the things I wanted to say and the tears that threatened to escape.

He smiled, and I swore the sun entered my small office. "Good. I will see you at Beans & Brews?" I nodded again, my lips pressed firmly together to hold the sobs in. He stood up and walked to the door, turning around once before leaving. "You look beautiful, Ivy." I died just a little. Why did he have to make this so hard?

Time crawled by, and I found myself checking the clock on my laptop every few minutes. Amber Lee had gone out of town and wouldn't come back until later that day. I needed to talk to someone who didn't judge me, who truly loved me for the ridiculous weakling I was. She was the only person in the world for that job. So I sat at my desk, fiddling with documents and not accomplishing anything until dinnertime rolled in. I grabbed my purse, a crossover small bag I had bought years ago at an arts & craft festival, and left the office.

It didn't take me long to get to the coffee shop. I walked in to the sound of a temple bell chime and searched the shop with my eyes. Li Qiang was sitting in a corner of the store at a two-person, round table. The restaurant was furnished in mismatched, salvaged furniture and decorated with amethyst-encrusted artwork, candles, and soothing paint compositions.

I sat across from him and tried to smile. "Did you order?"

He grinned. "Yes, today's special is your favorite, apple and Brie panini. Is that okay?" I nodded. He knew me better than my father, and we had only known each other for a few months. My stomach clenched at the thought of not having him in my life anymore. "You look pale. Are you feeling okay?"

Thankfully, the day had dawned cloudy, and the light didn't quite make it inside the bistro. Despite all the candles that had been lit to cut down the dimness, everything had still lost their sharpness and he couldn't see my swollen, wet eyes. "I'm fine. Just didn't sleep well last night."

Li Qiang reached over the table for my hand. "See?

You should have stayed at my place," he said, his voice an octave lower than before. "I know exactly what to do to make you sleepy." Parts of me tingled just as my heart broke even further.

"Li Qiang," I started, pulling my hand from under his and lowering my eyes, "you can stop the act now. It's over."

There was a moment of silence, and after a few seconds, I risked a glance. His beautiful eyes had narrowed to slits, and they were trained on me, his lips set in a straight line. "What act?"

"You pretending to be in love with me," I said quickly, afraid that if I didn't rush the words out, they would be stuck forever. "Us pretending we are in a real relationship." His grunt scared me more than anything else could. I wrung my hands on my lap, making myself look him in the eye. "I want to thank you for all you've done for me. You were amazing and almost made me believe it was real."

He swallowed a few times, his Adam's apple bobbing in his neck. "Almost? I *almost* made you believe it was real?" I had never heard that angry tone of voice from him, and it frightened me. "Do you think I would have made love to you if I didn't mean what I said? Do you think that little of me?"

I didn't have the chance to answer. Marcy, the witch who owned and ran the bistro, approached our table with our order. "Hi, lovely lovers," she said in her singsong voice. "Here are your sammies and drinks."

She turned her eyes to me and smiled, her fiery red hair creating a halo around her head. "I brought you this blue lace agate stone, Ivory." She held my hand in hers and placed a beautiful, light blue stone stripped in shades of blue and white in my palm, closing my fingers over it. "Keep it with you at all times, and it will help you." She winked at me, leaned over, and whispered in my ear, "Google it when you get home." And she was gone.

I stared at my fist for a while, not sure what to make of the witch's words. "Ivy." Li Qiang snapped me out of my thoughts. "Why do you think I was acting? I've always loved you. The story I told Teresa on air was not fictional. It was the honest truth. I became your intern so I could get to know you better and then fell in love with you. What makes you think I was putting on an act?"

Nobody had ever loved me like that. My father's words swam inside my head, swirling toxic thoughts that stained everything else. *You're not good enough. You're a disappointment. Who would ever love you? What self-respecting man would want you?* I was turning thirty-six in a couple of weeks, practically middle-aged. What would a brilliant and handsome twenty-seven-year-old want with me? How would he love me past the excitement of the novelty or when wrinkles marred my face and my skin began to sag?

"Li Qiang," I said, squeezing the stone in my hand, "I know you think you love me now, but I'm much older than you, and it wouldn't be right to hold you to it. Find a younger woman, someone who will grow old with you. Thank you for making me so very happy, even if it was for such a short time." I grabbed my bag and left, not wanting to find out what my sweet intern's face was showing. Better to leave him than having him leave me.

♥ ♥ ♥

"He did what?" Amber Lee's expression mirrored my own feelings even though, I supposed, I shouldn't be surprised. "Why? I thought he was happy here and that the two of you had hit it off." My friend had returned from her business trip late the night before, and I hadn't yet had the chance to tell her what had happened with Li Qiang.

It was on my desk when I first arrived to work that morning: Li Qiang's letter of resignation. I read it at least ten times, my mind reeling at the formality of its tone, as if we had been barely acquaintances. What did I expect though? It would have been extremely awkward to work together after what we had done— my face burned at the memories of some of the things. Beneath the crisp letter there was a note, which, however personal, was still distant and cold. *"Give me a call when you decide on when and how to make the announcement of our breakup to the staff. I will be there. As to my family, I will most likely tell them when*

I see them this weekend."

"It's over, Amber Lee." I couldn't take my eyes off the note. Despite what I had told him the day before, there was a finality to his words that my heart was having a hard time accepting. "The act, the ruse, whatever you want to call it."

Amber Lee gave me one of her are-you-freaking-crazy looks. "A ruse? Is that what you think the two of you were doing?" Her hands went up to her waist. "Maybe at first, yes, but for the past few weeks, that was no act; you're in love with him."

I sighed and slouched in my chair. "Yes, I am," I admitted, letting my head drop all the way until my forehead was on the note. "But he isn't."

She snorted. "Like hell he isn't," she said, slapping her hand on the desk, startling me up. "The man is so googly-eyed for you he must walk around all day with a permanent hard-on."

"Amber Lee!" I exclaimed, feigning outrage. "Physical attraction doesn't always translate into love. You know that."

My friend came around the desk and placed her hands on my shoulders. "Girl, I've known you my whole life. You are doing the same thing again." I looked up at her, my eyebrows arched high. "Don't look at me like that. You are sabotaging yourself again. It was bad enough with the other idiots you dated, but Li Qiang is a good man and he loves you. Don't do this to yourself."

"I'm not doing anything." As soon as I said it, I knew I was lying to myself. I loved Li Qiang with all my heart, but the whole thing was too good to be true, wasn't it? "Fairy tales are fiction, and Prince Charming just a figment of our romantic imagination."

Amber Lee gave me the look of death. "Shame on you. You run a business based on true love and finding your life partner, and you think that love doesn't really exist? I have never known you for a hypocrite."

I was about to reply when my phone vibrated on the table. It was a text message from Li Qiang: *"Don't believe what your father tells you. You are an incredible woman, and any man would be lucky to have you."* Like a fool, I stared at it, tears burning in my eyes and pain swelling in my chest. I grabbed my purse to get some tissues and something fell from it and rolled on the floor.

Amber Lee picked it up. "What's this?" She held the blue stone Marcy had given to me at the shop.

I opened the laptop and typed in "blue lace agate." An article in a trendy magazine read, "If you've been burned in the past or simply find the prospect of trusting someone very daunting, this pretty stone helps reduce your fear of rejection or making a wrong move and makes it easier for you to communicate your needs with a partner." I almost fell off the chair. How did Marcy know? We only knew each other in passing, and yet she had hit the nail on the head. I was scared of being disappointed again, scared of having my heart chewed and spit out like a piece of worthless gum. It wasn't that I didn't believe Li Qiang loved me; I was afraid to trick myself into a spot where only pain lurked.

I shut the laptop a bit too roughly and jumped to my feet. "Come with me," I said, not leaving any room for discussion. When my friend hesitated, I looped my arm through hers and pulled her toward the door. "We're going to see a witch."

Amber Lee expelled a funny little noise and followed me out. We sped through the busy streets, dodging people who balanced their to-go coffee cups in already overflowing hands. It didn't take long to get to Beans & Brews, just a couple blocks from my office. The place was jamming. Literally. There was a small crowd around the counter where Marcy's husband, a handsome, blind detective was handing out slices of toasted bread smothered in some type of berry jam. The small chalk board hanging on the wall behind the counter identified it as a mood-boosting jam made with blueberries and strawberries.

"Oliver, where's Marcy?" I yelled out over the chatter of the excited customers. Oliver lifted his head in greeting, his hands too busy to wave. "I need to talk to her."

"In the back, making more of these," he replied. "Go in, it's okay."

It felt weird to invade her space, but I was beyond reasonable thought at that point. All these nagging questions and doubts in my head demanded some kind of answer. I steered Amber Lee along with me around the counter to what I assumed was a small kitchen. It turned out it was so much more than that. The witch was bent over a short granite top counter, slathering jam on toast. Behind her, there was a cozy space, furnished with an overstuffed couch, a shaggy rug, and a quirky and colorful round table.

Marcy heard us walk in and looked up. "Hello, ladies." She didn't seem surprised in the least, as if it was totally normal for two almost-strangers to walk into her private space. "Take a sit. Let me take these to my husband, and we'll talk." She scooped the toast onto a large serving tray and carried it to the main store.

We sat on the edge of the couch, an old piece covered in soft blankets and cushions. "How do you think Marcy is going to help you? It's not like you need a love potion or anything. The man already loves you, and I don't think Marcy can fix your low opinion of yourself." I scowled at my best friend, despite the truth in her words.

Marcy was back before I could say anything. She smiled, adjusted the enormous polka-dot glasses on her nose, and sat on a small, tufted stool across from us. "I don't have a magic potion for what ails you, Ivory." My heart fell a bit. Not that I expected otherwise, but the romantic fool who lived inside of me was holding on to hope. "But I can give you some advice."

I leaned forward, supporting my arms on my knees. "Anything will be welcome." Amber Lee huffed beside me, and I threw her an evil look.

"Nothing you don't know already, but maybe you need to hear it from someone else." What did she mean by that? "You and my husband have a lot in common, you know." No, I didn't know. I knew Oliver in passing, but I had never really had a conversation with him. "I'll let him talk to you instead."

I made a move to stop her, but she had already waltzed out of the room. I turned to Amber Lee with a question in my eyes, and she shrugged. Oliver walked in, feeling the floor in front of him with his cane. He sat where Marcy had been a moment ago and smiled. He was a very handsome man with the most beautiful green eyes I had ever seen—blind eyes that seemed everything but.

"I apologize for my wife," he said, leaning his cane against the side of the stool. "In her wish to help, she sometimes forgets not everyone is comfortable sharing their demons."

All I had come to do was find out whether the quirky witch… what? What exactly was I looking for? "It's all right. I appreciate her trying to help, but we won't bother you anymore."

I gestured to Amber Lee to leave, but Oliver raised his hand. "Wait, Marcy is right about one thing; we do have a lot in common, you and me." Like what? I didn't even know him. "Marcy…" He searched for words. "My wife can see things no one else can. I'm sure you didn't tell her about your demons, but somehow she knows." That was creepy. What had I gotten myself into now? "Just like she saw mine a few years ago when I first met her. She knows that most of your problems come from an abusive father."

I was floored. How did he know that? I had never had that conversation with Marcy. Amber Lee cleared her throat and leaned forward.

Oliver chuckled. "No, she didn't divine that," he said. "She overheard you talking about your issues with your father during a few of your visits here." Holy shit. For a moment, I thought the red-haired witch was actually clairvoyant. "It's funny how people forget they're in a public place when it comes to coffee shops or restaurants. You wouldn't believe the things we hear while serving tea." My face burned. How mortifying. Oliver's smile died on his lips. "My father is a monster. He abused me both mentally and physically my whole life. He made me feel powerless, small, worthless." God, that sounded so familiar. I swallowed a sob. "Then I lost my sight, and I almost gave up on life altogether. I felt as if even God thought I was useless and unworthy."

My heart was having a battle inside of me, and my arms twitched with the urge to hug him. His words hit a chord. "What did you do?" I whispered.

"One day, I woke up and realized I was allowing my father to ruin my life." His eyes pierced me to the core, and I shivered, well-aware he couldn't see me. "Here I was a grown man, successful at what I did and still being manipulated by a father who loved no one but himself, a puppet in a monster's hands." He took a deep breath. "It wasn't easy, but from then on I cut myself off from my father's opinion of me. Anytime he put me down, I would stick metaphorical fingers in my ears and sing loudly so I couldn't hear him."

Marcy was right; this was nothing I didn't know already. I had long conversations with myself about that same subject. I needed to stop listening to my father, to stop believing what he said about me.

Oliver licked his lips and leaned closer to me, the table between us. He lowered his voice. "Don't let him control you, Ivory. Love who you are and don't believe a word he says." He sighed, pulling back. "I know he's your father and you want him to love you, but monsters are real and some of them share our genes. Just because he gave you life does not mean you have to obey him. Don't let his poison kill the beautiful soul you are."

Silence fell around us, and Amber Lee sought my hand and squeezed it. I gave her a pathetic, sad smile. "Thank you, Oliver. Thank you for sharing," I told him in a trembling voice. "Marcy was right; we do have a lot in common."

Oliver stood up, a giant of a man, and laughed. "Marcy is always right," he said. "I hope you come back soon with a lighter heart." He turned around and left the room, cane in hand.

"What are you going to do?" Amber Lee asked me in an uncharacteristically small voice, her hand still holding mine.

I turned my eyes to her. "I guess I must slay the beast."

CHAPTER EIGHTEEN

AN UNEXPECTED TWIST

"Come around ten on Thursday. I've called a staff meeting." My text to Li Qiang of a few days ago felt cold and cruel, but I was not sure what else to tell him. I had promised to let him know when he was needed to break the news to everybody else who thought we were still a couple. I kept my promises. But what I really wanted to tell him was how much I loved him and how much I wished we were still together. I shook my head and put the phone facedown on the desk.

I had been getting strange looks from my staff all morning. My dark mood of the last week or so was probably causing them to worry. I wouldn't be surprised if they thought I was about to fire a few of them. Actually, the TV appearance had been a great boon for the business and our customer pool had swelled up by at least 20 percent. The staff meeting

I had scheduled seemed to be a thorn in their side though, but I would put them out of their misery as soon as Li Qiang arrived.

Amber Lee, not certain either about what I was about to announce, had stopped at my favorite bakery and bought the whole place—at least, it looked that way when she arrived with boxes full of baked goods before anyone else was there. I made a large pot of coffee, and by ten o'clock I told everyone to stop their work and help themselves to the goodies. Li Qiang was not there yet, and I caught myself stealing glances at the clock on the wall every other minute or so. Where was he? I was nervous enough as it was without having to wonder whether he had decided not to show up.

By eleven, I decided to call him, but no one answered. I was beginning to worry. Even though Li Qiang was upset with me, he was not the kind of man to ignore my calls.

On impulse I called Li Wei and he picked up almost immediately. "Ivy? Why aren't you here yet?" Wei're's familiar voice made me smile.

"Here where?" I asked, wondering what he was going on about now. He was constantly sending me messages on the phone and making up excuses to come see me. I had become an expert at circumventing him.

"Where else?" He sounded annoyed… or maybe a little anxious. His voice had that shrillness I had witnessed that night after his nightmare. "In the hospital."

My heart stopped beating and all the blood drained out of my veins. A wall of ice descended on me. "Hospital? Who's sick?"

"Are you kidding me? Didn't he call you?" There was definite panic in his tone. "Li Qiang is in surgery. Why aren't you here?"

It was as if someone had punched the air out from me. "I didn't know. What hospital?"

Amber Lee sent everyone back to work, grabbed my purse, and stuffed me in her car while I tried to calm Li Wei down. The hospital was right around the corner. "He was riding his bike when it happened," he told me. "I guess it was so painful he fell off the bike and someone called 911. He called my parents from the ambulance."

"What's wrong with him?" Amber Lee navigated the crowded roads with the expertise of a race car driver and the language of a sailor.

"His appendix ruptured," Li Wei said. "He's in bad shape, Ivy." His voice shrunk to that of a much younger boy. "Why aren't you here yet?"

I swallowed my tears and tried to speak through my shallow breath. "He didn't call me, Wei're. I was waiting for him at work for a meeting. I didn't know." Why had he not called me? Was it because he thought I didn't care? Or because he hated me. "He'll be okay. I'm on my way. Five minutes."

Li Qiang must have been on his way to the office on his bike. Did people die from a ruptured appendix? I couldn't be sure, but I seemed to remember that it was a bad thing. A very bad thing. "Can you hurry, Amber Lee?"

"If I go any faster, we are going to take off," she mumbled, never taking her eyes off the road. "We're almost there. Is he okay?"

I shook my head. "I don't know. Appendicitis." I was having trouble talking or focusing on anything. What if he died? Oh my God, what if he died thinking I didn't love him? What was I thinking? What if he died period? I looked for a paper bag in her back seat. I was hyperventilating now.

"You need to calm down, Ivory," my friend said. "You're not going to help anyone if you freak out." I looked at her and began yoga breathing to calm myself down.

Amber Lee dropped me off at the ER and then drove away to go park the car. I ran inside on wobbly legs, oblivious to the commotion around me. I was standing in line to ask about Li Qiang when I heard my name. I turned around to find his mother by a vending machine. I left the line and rushed toward her.

"Mrs. Li, how is he? Is he okay?"

She grabbed my hands and patted them gently. "He's still in surgery," she said. Her hands trembled in mine. This was not good. "They'll know better after it. His appendix burst, and they're not sure how much bacteria has spread in his body."

Amber Lee arrived from behind us. "We came as

fast as we could."

Mrs. Li nodded. "No worries, I would have called you, but I thought Qiang'er had already done it."

I wasn't going to tell her we had broken up. "He might have," I lied. "We were very busy this morning and maybe I missed the call."

"I came to get a coffee, but the stupid machine is broke," Li Qiang's mom said, a sad, broken chuckle escaping with the words. "I really could use a cup of coffee."

Amber Lee stepped forward. "There's a Starbucks on the main lobby," she said. "I will get you all caffeinated. Who all wants coffee?" We made a tally and Amber Lee took off on her mission. She'd meet us all in the surgery family room.

Mrs. Li held on to me for dear life as we walked upstairs to the surgery ward. She was shaking so much I was afraid her legs wouldn't hold her. "Are you okay?"

She patted my hand again. "I'm fine. I have to be strong for Wei're, so I need to get my shakes under control." She looked up at me and smiled. "Our boy really likes you, you know. He'll be happy you're here."

As soon as her words left her lips, Li Wei came bounding down the hallway, yelling my name. "You're here, Ivy." He jumped into me and hugged me so fiercely I almost lost my balance. "I'm so glad you're here. Is my brother going to die?"

My heart skipped a beat. "Of course not, Wei're.

This happens all the time, and the doctors know exactly what to do." I hoped I wasn't lying. "He'll be giving you orders in no time, you'll see."

Both Mr. Li and their daughter came to greet me, and we all sat close together in the soft cushioned chairs of the waiting room. Amber Lee showed up not long after with a paper tray filled with coffee drinks. The flat white she had brought me slid down my throat in a hot wave of comfort. Li Qiang would be all right. He'd be fine.

A doctor emerged from the door, and we all hopped to our feet, huddling around her. "How's he doing?" was the question we all uttered at the same time.

The doctor, still in her scrubs, smiled. "He'll be fine. There was some leakage of pus, but we were able to control it and clean it out of his system," she said, triggering a loud, collective sigh. "We'll keep him for a couple days to make sure there are no complications, but he's healthy and strong. I envision no problems."

"When can we see him?" Mrs. Li asked, echoing my own thoughts.

"Family can go in and keep him company as soon as he's in his room." She threw me and Amber Lee a glance. "Anyone else, maybe tomorrow if his family allows."

Amber Lee shook her head. "It's okay, I don't have to go in, but Ivory…."

Mrs. Li held on to my arm. "Ivy is family," she said to the doctor. "She's my son's fiancée. She can go in with us."

Tears rose to my eyes. This woman who I barely knew was kinder to me than my own father. The mother of the man I had just broken up with because of my own demons saw me as family. Guilt filled and mixed with joy in my heart. "Thank you, Mrs. Li, but you don't have to do this."

She squeezed my arm. "Don't be silly. How could we not count you as family when my son loves you so much?"

I couldn't hold it any longer; I burst out crying.

Amber Lee came back an hour or so later with a basket full of sandwiches and sodas. They wouldn't let her in the room, so Li Wei and I went to the waiting room to pick them up. Li Qiang was still under the effect of the anesthesia, looking peaceful and beautiful like he always did. I told my friend to go home, that I would take an Uber later. The poor woman had been waiting around for a couple hours already, and the phone had been ringing constantly with calls from my staff, all worried sick about Li Qiang. "Better go back to the office and put everybody's mind to rest," I told her. "They won't get anything done if they are worried."

After she left, we returned to the room with the sandwiches. Now that he knew his brother was going to be okay, Li Wei's appetite was back with a vengeance, and his sandwich didn't quite make it to the room. As soon as we opened the door, we knew something had happened; there was an almost festive atmosphere with lots of chatter filling the air.

Li Fang came dashing toward me. "He's awake," she said, holding my hand and pulling me. I only had time to put the box of sandwiches on a nearby table before being whisked close to the bed.

Li Qiang was indeed awake, his eyes narrowed and a drunken smile on his lips. "What's the party for?" he asked, speech slightly slurred. "Is it my birthday?" Everybody chuckled.

Mrs. Li threw a delighted glance at her husband before sitting on the edge of the bed and holding her son's hands. "You're finally awake, *háizi*. You worried us all sick." She brought his hand to her lips, being careful not to bother the IV. "How are you feeling?"

"I feel drunk," he said with a guffaw. "What did I drink, Mom?"

Mr. Li laughed. "You're still woozy from the anesthesia, son. You had a burst appendix."

"Oh, so that's what it was," Li Qiang said, closing his eyes and licking his lips. "I'm thirsty." Li Fang rushed to pick up the large glass of water the nurse had left for him, and he took long sips through the straw. "I fell from the bike."

He had some road burns from falling off his bike, but the doctors said that he must have been going pretty slow; there were no broken bones or wounds.

His unfocused eyes roamed the small crowd

surrounding his bed and eventually landed on me. "Ivy?" My stomach flip-flopped. "Why are you here?"

Everybody turned their eyes to me. "I was worried," I said, feeling pathetic. "I wanted to make sure you're okay. Do you want me to leave?"

Mrs. Li stood up and turned to me. "Don't be silly, girl. We will all go for some fresh air so you two can talk." I opened my mouth to protest, but she shook a hand and shooed everyone out of the room. "Take your time."

Suddenly we were alone—me and the man I loved, the man I had broken up with just a few days before. My face and neck burned. I swallowed and asked again, "Do you want me to leave?"

He shook his head slowly, his eyes closed again. "I'm glad you're here," he whispered. "Have you told them?"

"Your parents?" He nodded. "No, of course not."

"Good." He was quiet for a moment; then he opened his eyes. "I'm very sleepy. Can you lay down with me?"

I was not sure the hospital staff would be happy about that, but I couldn't say no. Trying not to mess with the tubes and cables that connected him with the IV and the monitors, I took off my shoes and slid on top of the bed, next to him. "Is this okay?"

He swung his hand across his body to hold my hand and turned his face to mine. I could feel his warm breath on my lips, and tears pooled in my eyes. I didn't want to break up with him. I loved him.

Li Qiang closed his eyes again, touched his dry lips briefly against mine, and whispered, "*Wǒ ài nǐ,* Ivy. I love you." His breathing slowed, and I knew he was asleep. Only then did I allow the tears to roll down my cheeks.

"What have I done, Xiǎoli?" I whispered, my lips almost touching his. "I love you so much."

I brushed my fingers across his brow and then down his temple and cheek. He looked so young, lying there, slumber relaxing every muscle on his face, his eyes black crescents against his pale skin. I wanted to spend the rest of my life with that man. I wanted to be the reason he rushed home after work and stayed up every night. Why had I allowed my demons, my father's voice, to control me? To scare me so much I had given up on the dream of a lifetime: finding love, real love.

My father was right after all; I was really stupid.

CHAPTER NINETEEN

MAKING AMENDS

"Amber Lee, can you come here please?" I yelled out from my desk, too lazy to press the intercom button on my phone. It was a pretty small office, so unless there were customers present, we didn't stand on ceremony.

A few seconds later, my friend stuck her head in the doorway. "You called, boss?" She gave me one of her wicked smirks, and I was tempted to forget my age and stick my tongue out at her.

"I'm going out for a bit," I told her, closing the laptop and getting up. "I am meeting a client at Beans & Brews, and then I may have to run an errand."

She tilted her head and looked at me sideways. "You're up to something." She knew me too well, my awesome childhood friend. "What are you not telling me?"

I had to laugh. "Damn, woman. Can't hide anything

from you." I grabbed my straw bag. "I'm meeting with my father for lunch."

For once I had the satisfaction of watching my friend's expression turn from amused to shocked. "What?" She scanned me from head to toe. "You're not dressed...." I knew what she meant; I wasn't dressed the way I normally did for meetings with my father. I was wearing my regular boho-style trappings, a long burnt-yellow linen dress with large, white daisies printed on the bottom edge—not at all what my father would deem professional. "Really?"

I smiled again. "Yes, I am meeting with him," I said, grabbing her arm and pulling her with me to the main office. "I will no longer cater to his idea of professionalism." Her eyes widened. "If he doesn't like what he sees, then too bad." I was planning on donating the couple "professional" outfits I had bought just for such meetings. "Oliver was right. I gotta stop trying to please a man who will never be pleased with anything I do. I'm pretty sure he would still have some biting remark if I won a Nobel prize." I laughed at my own joke, and for once there wasn't any bitterness in my words.

Amber Lee grasped my arm tightly. "You'll call me afterward, right?" I nodded. "Are you coming back to the office at all today?"

"Yes, and stop fretting," I told her, giving her a brief hug. "I'm fine, better than ever." I was. Marcy was right. I needed to hear it from someone else, somebody who knew how it felt, how it made you doubt every thought, every action. Another soul who had struggled with his sense of self-worth, who hated who he was and how he felt. After that conversation, I decided that, like Oliver, I wasn't going to be a victim anymore; I'd be a survivor instead.

My meeting with the customer at Beans & Brews went well, and I had some time to kill afterward, so I sat at the small table, sipping Marcy's delicious Cream Earl Grey and munching on lavender mini scones. The witch had some mad culinary skills. The place was busy as always but never lost its soothing atmosphere. With as many patrons coming in and out, getting their midmorning caffeine or sugar fix, the whole place kept its serene quietness.

"A penny for your thoughts?" The pretty red-haired witch stood by the table, large, yellow and white spectacles hanging precariously on her tiny nose.

I smiled. "What? You can't read my thoughts?"

Marcy laughed and sat on the chair across from mine. "I'm working on that skill, but it's hard," she said, wrinkling her nose. She looked at me for a moment before asking, "How are you doing?"

I sought her hand on top of the table and gave it a squeeze. "I'm great, thank you." Letting go of her, I dug in my dress pocket and pulled out the stone she had given me. I held it aloft between us. "This damned thing works." We both giggled. "Please, tell that sexy husband of yours I am very thankful for what he shared with me. It really made a difference. I've been so beaten down, I never stopped to think that there were others out there with the same problem."

"Oliver is a good man," she said with that great smile of hers. "And you are a fabulous woman—strong, beautiful, and successful." She stood up. "Go get them!"

I paid her for the food and left the shop with a lightness in my chest I hadn't felt in a long time or at all. I got in my car and drove across town to the pretentious little French restaurant my father so favored. He was already sitting at the usual table, his back straight as a rod, a beautiful iceberg in the ocean of my life. I sighed and sat next to him.

"Ivory," he said as if reminding me of my own name. His eyes roamed my body, disapproval in the curve of his lips. "Did you go to work dressed like that?"

I laughed and opened a napkin over my lap. "Yes, isn't it a lovely dress? It makes me happy when I wear it." His jaw dropped, and he seemed lost for words. "It's like wearing a warm, bright, sunny spring day."

Just as he opened his mouth to say something, the waiter approached to get our orders. I ordered a salad, and my father took some time placing his complicated custom order—a man used to having his way. My heart hurt, but the bleeding had stopped finally.

"What are you going to do about your Asian boy?" Not man, not boyfriend, but a mere boy. He had a gift to make words mean so much more than their face value. "Do you insist on continuing this public charade? You'll lose clientele, you know."

"How, Father? How am I going to lose clientele because I date a younger, Asian man?" I asked, not a note of sarcasm in my tone. "Please, enlighten me because I can't figure it out."

My father wiped an imaginary crumb from his lip with the corner of the napkin. "You've always been a bit dumb, Ivory." The barbs were out. "You want to attract the elite, that's where money is. And the elite in this town doesn't want to be mixed up with immigrants."

I took a moment to bury the anger his words always stirred in me. "First, Li Qiang and his family are not immigrants. His family has been in the US for as long as ours," I said, my voice calm and cool. "Second, I'm not interested in attracting what you call the elite, especially not the ones who are bigots and classists. They are very welcome to take their business elsewhere." There was a new fire burning inside me, and it felt as good as it hurt. "And third, Father, there is nothing wrong with being an immigrant. If I recall correctly, you come from a family of French immigrants yourself." I pretended to be thinking for a moment. "Yes, the Tower family came to the United States from Tour in northern France sometime around the early 1800s and settled in New York. Our family were of poor, uneducated backgrounds looking for a way to make a decent living. You taught me this, so

I don't understand why you'd be so down on modern immigrants."

My father had turned a sickly shade of red. I had never seen him like that, and for a moment I worried he was having a heart attack. Then I remembered the man had no heart.

"I came today," I said, dropping my napkin beside my empty charger, "to tell you that we should keep these lunch or dinner meetings to maybe once a year." Now that the words were rolling, there was no stopping me. "If you absolutely need to demean or chide me, you can always just send me a phone message or email. No need to do it face-to-face." He opened his mouth, but I cut him off again. "So let's make this lunch the last one for a long while, Father. I don't wish you ill, so take good care of yourself." I stood up to leave. "And if you ever decide to use a dating site, please don't use mine. I only accept clients with a heart. Feel free to eat my salad."

As I walked out of the restaurant, something inside me broke free. The weight I had been carrying around for thirty-six years had lifted, and it felt so good.

"You're crazy." Amber Lee was probably right, but I was determined. She threw her arms up in the air in defeat. "Okay, I'll set it up on my side. Just be ready to go when it's time."

I smiled and went back to my work, the laptop

glowing in the semidarkness of my office. The day had dawned cloudy, and even though it was almost nine in the morning, the sun was still struggling to shine through the covering.

My friend stopped by the door and turned halfway. "You're not going to break his heart, are you?" I gave her the you-know-me-better-than-that glare, and she left.

I had been thinking about this since I visited the hospital two days ago when Li Qiang had surgery. They were keeping him one extra day because the doctors wanted to make sure the antibiotic he was on was doing what it was supposed to do, so today would be the perfect occasion to do what I was planning. Since we hadn't had the staff meeting because of the surgery, I was going to bring it to him at the hospital bed.

The meeting with my father the day before had changed me. I couldn't say years of emotional abuse had been erased from my mind, but my confidence had most certainly swelled, and I was willing to accept that I was worthy of being properly loved. For someone who had spent the last twenty years or so denying herself the joy of being cared for, that was major progress.

I finished my work as quickly as I could, packed my laptop, and left the office. I wanted to stop at a flower shop on the way to the hospital. Marcy had also asked me to stop by because she had a special tea to send to Li Qiang. "It's very healing and soothing," she promised.

By the time I arrived at the hospital, I had a large thermos inside my straw bag, the laptop bag hanging from my shoulder, and two flower bouquets in my hands. Instead of the more conservative dresses I normally wore to work, I had put on a pair of jeans, a white top, and a translucent blue-print duster. I had contemplated wearing high heels, but considering the run around I had to do, I settled on plain white sneakers.

Li Wei was waiting for me in the lobby. "Ivy, did you buy the whole flower shop?" Cheeky monkey. Instead of rewarding him with a sarcastic response, I handed him one of the bouquets.

"That one is for your mom," I told him, plucking a fallen petal from one of the red roses. I hesitated for a moment. "Wei're, red means happiness and good luck, right?"

The boy nodded, sticking his nose in the roses and taking a long sniff. "These smell good. My mom will like them."

We got in the elevator and emerged in the ward where Li Qiang had been taken after recovery. As soon as Wei're saw his mother talking to a doctor by the nurse's station, he took off running. "Mom, Mom, look at the flowers Ivy brought for you."

Mrs. Li was still smelling them, a smile stretched across her lips, when I reached her. "Oh, Ivy, these are so pretty. Thank you so much. You're a sweetheart."

I leaned over and planted a kiss on her cheek. "Thank you for bringing up such a great son," I told her. I threw Li Wei a sideways glance. "And a good little monkey too." Wei're play smacked me on the arm. "I'm kidding, Wei're. You're a good son too."

We talked for a few minutes while the young boy chased a nurse who had promised him some pudding. Li Fang soon joined us, a Starbucks coffee in her hand. "Qiang'er will kill me if I drink this in front of him," she said with a chuckle. "The doctor told him no coffee for a few days."

"Is he doing okay?" They nodded, but I saw the question in their eyes. "I had something rather important to do yesterday, so I couldn't come. But I hope you don't mind, Mrs. Li, I'm holding a special staff meeting in a little while."

Mrs. Li's eyes rounded, brows arched. "You're leaving?"

I shook my head. "No, no, it's a virtual staff meeting. I called in the staff on a Saturday so Li Qiang can be part of it," I explained, pointing at my laptop. "Amber Lee is running it from the office."

"Something serious happened?" Li Fang asked.

"Nothing serious, just an announcement I must make," I admitted. "You are welcome to be in the room with us. Is Mr. Li here?"

"Bao had to work today, but he'll be here later."

There was no more delaying. I had about fifteen minutes tops before the meeting was supposed to start. "Can I talk to Li Qiang alone first?" I asked.

Mrs. Li touched my hand and smiled. "Of course,

sweetie. Go ahead. Just let us know when you want us to come in." Li Wei's voice announced his return even before we could see him. His mom added, "Don't worry, I will hold the little monster here. Go."

I knocked on the door lightly before walking in. My handsome intern was propped up on a couple pillows, staring at the window as if watching TV. He turned his eyes to me as I walked in. "Hi, Xiǎoli." Nerves were taking over, and I couldn't be sure I spoke out loud.

"Ivy." There was no smile, and for a moment all I wanted to do was turn around and flee. "How are you?"

Glad I had worn flat shoes, I walked on my shaky legs until I was next to his bed. "I brought you flowers." What a dumb thing to say. I now knew exactly how Baby felt in *Dirty Dancing*. "I hope you like them."

Li Qiang gave the flowers a cursory look and nodded. "They're beautiful, thank you." I stuck them in a vase the nurse had left on the nightstand. "Why are you here?" There was no warmth in his voice, and my heart shrank. Was I too late?

"I promised you I would hold a staff meeting to make an announcement," I said, choked. I slid the laptop bag on the bed and unzipped it. "We're starting in five minutes."

He was quiet at first while I set up the computer, keeping my head down and avoiding his eyes. "You couldn't wait until I went home?"

I swallowed, my mouth as dry as the Sahara Desert. "This is important, so I thought I might as well get it done." I knew what he was thinking. How could I not? But I had high hopes that he would forgive me. "Sorry I didn't come yesterday."

"Why would you?" His voice was cold, so unlike the one I was used to. "It's not like we have a relationship or anything."

I took a deep breath and turned on the laptop. "I went to see my father." I looked up at him, curious to see his reaction and was rewarded with a sharp intake of air. "I won't be seeing him anymore. His reign of terror is over." I let out a bitter chuckle at my terrible attempt at a joke.

Li Qiang grabbed my wrist. "Are you okay?" Concern tinted his voice. I sighed and nodded. "I'm proud of you," he added, letting go of my hand. "You're too good for him."

The screen lit up. "Are you ready?" I made the connection, and a picture of our office and all our staff materialized. "Good morning to you all from Li Qiang's bedside." There were some chuckles and a wave of hellos. Even Li Qiang managed a smile. "As you all know, I have an important announcement to make. And no, no one is being fired." I laughed nervously. "It's more of a personal matter."

I stood up and went to the door to let Mrs. Li and her kids in the room. "I have you all here today to set things straight. You all know that Li Qiang and I were dating." A buzzing of voices rippled through the air. "Well, the truth is that we really weren't." The surprise was virtually palpable, but other than a few gasps everyone was quiet. "I had cornered myself in a tight spot—a long story for another time—and Li Qiang helped me out by pretending he was my boyfriend."

Li Wei stepped forward. "Does that mean you guys are not dating?" I shook my head. "But you kissed and all that." Heat rose to my cheeks. "You were faking it?"

"Yes, Wei're, we were faking it." I chanced a glance at Li Qiang. His mouth was set in a straight line, and his knuckles had turned white as his fingers closed on the edge of the blanket. "But then something unexpected happened." Every bit of noise was sucked into silence. "I fell in love with him for real."

Li Qiang raised his eyes to me, his lips parting slightly. I smiled at him and then at Li Wei who was still hovering beside me.

"I fell so hard in love with him it scared me shitless," I continued, returning my gaze to my boyfriend. "I was terrified that he would eventually leave me, so I decided to be proactive and just end the relationship before it even started."

Mrs. Li came from behind and placed her hands on my shoulders. "*Shǎ gūniáng*, silly girl. My boy is so in love with you, he would never break your heart."

I covered one of her hands with mine and twisted around to look at her. "I know that now, Mrs. Li. I want nothing more than to date your son for real this time."

Li Qiang hadn't said anything, and my stomach was

brewing something caustic. I reached out for his hand, afraid he would recoil. He didn't. He loosened his grip on the sheets and wrapped his large hand around mine. "Will you forgive me, Xiǎoli? I love you."

He still didn't say a word. Instead, he pulled me closer and kissed me.

CHAPTER TWENTY

WŎ ÀI NĬ

"You're trying to kill me, aren't you?" It was the usual daily complaint. Li Qiang hated our daily walks around the block, but it was what the doctor ordered. My boyfriend claimed the wound was still too sore and that making him walk everyday was pure torture. Personally, I thought he actually loved it.

"What are you complaining about?" I replied, helping him out of his light jacket. "We even got to stop at Beans & Brews to drink Marcy's healing tea."

He frowned, sticking his tongue halfway out of his mouth. "Eww, that's the worst tasting tea I have ever drank." I laughed. "If it wasn't for the fact I think it actually helps with the healing, I'd never touch it again."

Li Qiang sat on the nearest couch, and I went to the kitchen to put away the few groceries we had bought on the way home. "But you also drank coffee today, so that's a bonus, right?" He had been off the caffeine since the surgery, three weeks ago, but his surgeon had finally given him the green light.

"Come sit with me, *gūniáng*." He patted the seat next to him. I closed the fridge door and came to sit by him, nestling my head on the crook of his neck and shoulder. "I'm glad you're willing to torture me every day in order to heal me." I chuckled. "But can you be gentler sometimes? I'm a bit fragile right now."

I raised my head to look at his pretend pout. "You're so full of shit," I said, slapping his chest playfully. "The doctor said one more week, and you should be good to go. Fragile my ass."

He gave me a wicked sideways glance. "You have a fine ass, Tower *gūniáng*. Among other fine parts." He winked, and I huffed, feigning outrage. He pulled me back to his shoulder. "I love that you're here with me, Ivy. Thank you."

"Don't thank me yet. You haven't seen my bill," I quipped, inhaling his subtle citrus scent. I had been staying with him since his hospital discharge. Mrs. Li had enough to do with a ten-year-old at home to be taking care of her oldest son too, and I loved being near him, even when he drove me crazy with demands: "I need to go to the bathroom," "I'm thirsty," "It's too cold." After the first week, I made sure he understood he needed to do all those things by himself with minimal help from me, even if secretly I was more than happy to do it.

"I think I'll take a nap," he said after a moment of silence. "That walk pooped me out."

"It's not even eleven in the morning, Xiǎoli." I straightened and twisted my body to face him. "You don't need a nap."

He winked, and his luscious lips curved into a beautiful smile. "Well, a nap with benefits that is." Wicked man.

"Too early for sex. It's only been three weeks."

"My wound is healed, and the doctor told me I could go back to my regular life with moderation." He stood up, groaning a little. No matter what he said, there was still some residual soreness on his right side. He grabbed my hand and pulled me up. "I need some TLC." The momentum threw me into his arms. He leaned down and kissed me, his lips prying mine apart and his tongue sliding between them. He tasted so good, I closed my eyes and allowed myself a moment of abandon. "I want to carry you to my bed, but I think the doctor might frown upon it."

I chuckled, heat rushing through every inch of my body. "I'll carry you," I said, knowing all too well I was not strong enough. "In my dreams, that is. Just walk with me, then."

I held tightly to his hand and pulled him toward the room, not sure it was the best idea. I was terrified his stitches would snap open. The surgeon had told us he had been very lucky because they had opened him up just in time to stop the bacteria from spreading inside him. He'd be walking around with a packed wound if that wasn't the case. He had taken antibiotics until recently, and he did seem to be in perfect health, but I didn't want to push it.

For someone who had just spent the last half hour complaining about how much it hurt to walk around the block, Li Qiang was certainly spry as he sauntered to the room with me in tow. I chuckled under my breath. Priorities, I guessed.

We fell on the bed, entangled in each other, our lips and bodies glued together. "God, I miss this," he whispered over my opened lips, his hand sneaking under my T-shirt and cupping my breast. "You feel and taste amazing, *gūniáng*."

I pushed him away for a moment. "What exactly does that mean, *gūniáng*?" He had told me a while back that it meant "girl," but now that I had been around him for a while and heard him speak in Chinese with his parents, I was wondering if there wasn't a hidden meaning attached to it. Good thing I trusted him, because for all I knew he could be calling me something pretty nasty.

He rolled on his back, arms spread eagle, and laughed. "I thought you knew." I shook my head, half sitting, half lying on my side. "It just means girl. It's kind of a respectful term for a young, unmarried woman."

"What? That's all?" I exclaimed. "I thought it

meant 'my love' or something like that."

He turned to his side and laid his hand on my hip, his half-closed eyes flirty and sensual. "No, that'd be *wǒ de ài*," he said, scooting closer, his hand rubbing the exposed skin of my waist. "I was waiting for our wedding to call you that." My eyes rounded in surprise. He laughed softly. "But I guess there's no time like the present, right?"

He sat up and pressed his lips to mine, gently at first but progressively hungrier, his warmth and taste creating havoc with my senses. He pulled my T-shirt over my head and threw it to some undisclosed spot in the room, not wasting any time to unclasp my bra and thrusting it the same way. When his mouth closed around my breast, I moaned, my head thrown back as his touch made every inch of my body glow in pleasure.

Switching gears, my boyfriend trailed kisses from my breast all the way to my lips again. "*Wǒ de ài*," he whispered, his lips vibrating against mine. "*Wǒ ài nǐ.*"

I tilted my neck backward to give him easier access as he pampered me with hot kisses. "What's that?" I knew it, but I wanted to hear him say it again.

"I love you," he said, his fingers fumbling with the button on my shorts. I stopped him. "What's wrong?"

I slid off the bed, his face turning into panic mode. "You are still recovering from emergency surgery, so I insist on taking care of you." His thick dark brows knitted together. I gave him a lopsided smile. "Are you worried?"

I climbed over the bed, kneeled by him, and began unzipping his jeans. His brow smoothed out in comprehension. When I hovered over him to unbutton his shirt, he cupped both my breasts with his hands. Heat pooled in my most intimate parts, and I moaned. After that, I made haste to remove all his clothing. My boyfriend was gorgeous, lying there naked as the day he was born, lean muscle in all the right places. Lower on his right hip, right above and almost parallel with his Adonis belt, his scar was a faded shade of red. I kissed it gently, aware it was still tender to the touch.

Li Qiang groaned. "See? Still trying to kill me." His smile belied his words. "But now that you started it, I hope you finish it."

I kissed his scar again, tracing the bump of his Adonis belt from the area just below the waist all the way down his pelvis. I ran the palm of my hand over his hardness, a barely there caress, taking my time and enjoying his squirming. My lips soon replaced my hand, latching and sliding along his length, my tongue brushing over his velvety skin. He moaned, and I intensified my efforts until it was clear he wouldn't last much longer. Under protest, I slipped off the bed again and got rid of my shorts and undies, pausing only for a quick run to the bedside table for a condom.

Slowly, I unrolled the prophylactic on him. Li Qiang lifted his upper body on his elbows, but I pushed him down again. This was going to happen with minimum straining on his part, I had decided, so

I straddled him. In a quick move, I lifted my bottom and then brought myself down, burying him inside me. "You don't move, you hear?" I told him, choked by the mounting pressure in my core. "I'll do all the work."

I rocked back and forth on top of him, careful not to put my full weight on his scar, and brought us both to the brink in no time. We both exploded seconds apart. Afraid to hurt him, I rolled off him right away and stretched beside him, my hand on his chest.

"Xiǎoli," I whispered, breathless and sated. "*Wǒ ài nǐ.*"

He turned his face to me, as breathless as me, and smiled. "I love you too, *wǒ de ài,* I love you too. "

♡ ♡ ♡

Teresa Lord was like always: flawless in her hairstyle, makeup, and clothing. She held her microphone like a scepter and smiled at the TV audience like the sovereign she was. A gentle breeze kept the temperature of the warm air just right. The TV anchor stood at the end of the red carpet, reminding me of a Hollywood reporter covering the Oscars, except this was no Cali and I wasn't receiving an Oscar.

I stood in front of the body-length mirror and watched Teresa from a distance, straining to hear what she was saying while Amber Lee adjusted my long, white, skintight dress. "Can you stand still for a second?" she mumbled irritably. "Can you even breathe in this dress?" She fumbled with the back clasps and cursed profusely.

The soft, melodic sound of Teresa's voice reached me in spurts. "Local business owner… dating service… her day has come… Prince Charming." I chuckled, and Amber gave me a dirty look. "A success story… matched numerous couples… loving relationships… her turn."

"God only knows what story she's weaving," I told my friend who had finally stood up to face me. She smiled and spun me slowly so I could see myself in the mirror. My dress had a beautiful lace-lined bodice with a neckline that plunged down between my breasts, cinched at the waist from where a flowing, multilayered, plain white skirt bloomed. I had decided to forgo any head dressing and allowed my own brown, wavy mane to cascade over my lace-covered shoulders. I loved the dress, simple and gorgeous.

"You look beautiful, my friend," Amber Lee said, clasping her hands in delight. "Li Qiang won't know what hit him." I laughed along with her.

The sound of a violin interrupted our moment of levity. It was time. "Here goes nothing," I said and froze. Mr. Li was at the door, looking dapper in a tuxedo. "Mr. Li? What's wrong?"

My fiancé's father smiled. "Absolutely nothing. You look beautiful," he said. Then he stretched a hand toward me. "Will you give me the honor of letting me walk you down the aisle?"

Tears pooled in my eyes. I couldn't cry now or I would be a raccoon bride. My own father was not invited since I didn't want this moment of happiness marred by his presence, but I'd never expected Mr. Li to do this. I swallowed my tears and walked toward him, wrapping my hand around his. "Of course, thank you so much."

Mr. Li placed my hand on his forearm and patted it. "Sweetheart, maybe this will inspire Li Fang to marry that old boyfriend of hers and leave the house." He laughed, and I did this weird thing with my mouth that came out as half sob, half chuckle. "Let's take you to my son before he loses patience and comes to get you himself."

With my arm looped through his, we walked out of the makeshift dressing room—just a glorified tent in the back of the Li's garden—and onto the red carpet. The violin was joined by another and a cello, and my heart leaped in my chest as my eyes found my groom. Li Qiang was at the other end of the runner, looking every inch the beautiful soul he was in his modern, simple black tuxedo. My lips stretched wide, and I fought the urge to propel myself down the path into his arms, damn tradition and decorum. As if guessing my thoughts, my soon-to-be father-in-law pressed his hand over my arm and smiled.

The music carried me on floating feet until I was face-to-face with the man I wanted to spend the rest of my life making love to. His smile reflected my own, and his eyes were suspiciously shiny. I wasn't the only one getting emotional, after all. He reached for my hand and whispered, "Are you ready for this?"

"Are you ready, Ivy?" My smile turned to a frown as someone shook my shoulder. "Ivy? Wake up, *gūniáng.* We have to get ready to go."

Slowly I woke up from the dream, my eyes opening to find my man's beautiful face staring at me with an amused turn of his lips. I groaned. It was all a dream.

"Wow, did I wake you up from a dream where you were on a date with Chris Pratt or something?" He leaned back on the pillow and crossed his arms, feigning jealously.

I shook my head, stretched, and scooted closer to him, my arm draped over his chest. He was wearing his penguin pajamas, and I chuckled, nuzzling the soft fabric. "No, I was marrying you."

He pulled me up so he could look me in the eye. "You were dreaming of our wedding?" I nodded, sleepy laziness still attached to all my bones. "How was it?"

I yawned. "It was beautiful. I was wearing the dress of my dreams." I laughed at my own pun. "And your dad walked me down the aisle. So sweet."

He was quiet for a moment. "Do you want to?" I lifted a brow. "Get married? I mean, I haven't asked you yet."

I pouted. "Yeah, why haven't you?" I teased him. "I'm a middle-aged woman; I don't want to walk down the aisle in a walker."

He laughed and pressed me closer to him. "If that's the case, I will just carry you," he said. "But you are far from old, Ivy."

I lifted my head and planted a kiss on his chin. "Good that you think so." A thought assailed me. "Xiǎoli, what will be my married name? Li Ivory?"

He snorted. "Only if you want to. In Chinese tradition, you keep your maiden name."

I thought about it for a moment. "The name Tower never really suited me anyway. Li Ivory or Ivory Li, western style, sounds a lot better, don't you think?"

"No matter what name you pick, you will always be Ivy, *wǒ de ài*. My love."

We lay in silence for a few minutes, enjoying each other's warmth. It had been almost two months since Li Qiang's surgery, and he was totally recovered. After much discussion, we decided he should follow his own career, and he had snagged an interview with a well-respected company for a high-paid position. He was not worried, nothing much seemed to worry my boyfriend, but I was anxious. That inner critic still accused me of being guilty of holding him back in his career.

"Do you want to get married, Ivy?" His voice was so serious, I sat up to better see him. "I know I want to spend the rest of my life with you, but I also know you're still sorting some things in your life."

I brushed my fingers on his cheek. "I do want to be your wife—shit, I already know what I'll be wearing." We laughed. "But you're right, I need a little time to clean up my head, get rid of all the voices, get used to loving myself for the first time."

He huffed. "Now I'm jealous," he joked. "I have to compete with yourself for your love? Not fair."

"You already have my love, silly." As if to prove it, I latched my lips to his in a long kiss. "See? I can't kiss myself like that."

Li Qiang snorted. "So what do we do? When will I know it's the right time to ask you to marry me?"

My heart sang; everything about Li Qiang made me happy. His voice soothed me, the warmth of his skin comforting and exciting at the same time, his kiss a powerful aphrodisiac. Even his flaws made me happy. Why would I ever not want to marry him? I had a feeling it would happen a lot sooner than even I thought. But not yet.

"Xiǎoli, what about if I just assume you want to ask me, and *I* ask you instead?" His brow furrowed and then smoothed out as his wicked smile appeared. "Will that work?"

He didn't have to answer. The touch of his lips against mine, the waltz of our tongues, and the pressure of his hand cupping the back of my neck was clear. I would be his wife one day soon.

ACKNOWLEDGEMENTS

All my thanks go to the usual crew who either supported me emotionally (my cheerleaders) or professionally: my family, my friends, my library critique group, and the fabulous team at Hot Tree Self-Publishing.

To my writer friends who I only know in cyber-space goes a huge shoutout of appreciation; you have been amazing, always willing to listen, advise, cheer on, and lend a hand.

To the Taiwanese lady (who chose to remain anonymous) who helped me with the Chinese Mandarin language, thank you so much.

The beta readers who made me feel like a million dollars with their kind comments and reactions, I love you guys!

Last, but not least, a big thank you to my followers. Without you my stories would never leave my laptop. Love you all, fabulous readers!

This story is the product of a year of the pandemic. Writing it definitely helped me keep positive. I hope it brings a note of joy and lots of smiles to you too.

保重 (Bǎozhòng), aka take care.

If you liked **DATING THE INTERN** you might want to check out Natalina Reis's other books.

ROMANTIC COMEDY:

WE WILL ALWAYS HAVE THE CLOSET
books2read.com/closet

LOVED YOU ALWAYS
books2read.com/lovedyoualways

BLIND MAGIC
books2read.com/blindmagic

HER REAL MAN
/books2read.com/realman

FICTIONAL-ISH
books2read.com/fictional-ish

DYSTOPIAN ROMANCE:

HEART'S PREY
books2read.com/hearts-prey

MM PARANORMAL ROMANCE:

LAVENDER FIELDS
books2read.com/lavenderfields

Infinite Blue
books2read.com/infinite-blue

Of Magic & Scales
books2read.com/ofmagicandscales

Of Scales & Fire
books2read.com/ofscalesandfire

Of Fire & Bone
books2read.com/offireandbone

FM PARANORMAL ROMANCE:

Dark Feathers
books2read.com/darkfeathers

ROMANTIC FANTASY:

Desert Jewel
books2read.com/desertjewel

Snow Jewel
books2read.com/snow-jewel

Rebel Jewel
books2read.com/rebel-jewel

AUTHOR'S BIO

Natalina wrote her first romance in collaboration with her best friend at the age of 13. Since then she has ventured into other genres, but romance is first and foremost in almost everything she writes.

After earning a degree in tourism and foreign languages, she worked as a tourist guide in her native Portugal for a short time before moving to the United States. She lived in three continents and a few islands, and her knack for languages and linguistics led her to a master's degree in education. She lives in Virginia where she has taught English as a Second Language to elementary school children for more years than she cares to admit.

Natalina doesn't believe you can have too many books or too much coffee. Art and dance make her happy and she is pretty sure she could survive on lobster and bananas alone. When she is not writing or stressing over lesson plans, she shares her life with her husband and two adult sons.

FOLLOW NATALINA ON SOCIAL MEDIA

FACEBOOK
www.facebook.com/authornatalinareis

WEBSITE/BLOG
www.natalinareis.com

TWITTER
www.twitter.com/TichaB

GOODREADS
www.goodreads.com/author/show/14883335.Natalina_Reis

AMAZON
www.amazon.com/Natalina-Reis/e/B01ADQ9FJW/

BOOKBUB
www.bookbub.com/profile/natalina-reis

INSTAGRAM
www.instagram.com/reisnatalina

READER'S GROUP
www.facebook.com/groups/215263965917134

PINTEREST
www.pinterest.com/lisboeta62